BOSS WITH BENEFITS

MICKEY MILLER

Edited by
DANIELLE BECKETT
Edited by
VIRGINA CAREY

MILLER MEDIA, LLC

Copyright © 2017 by Mickey Miller

All rights reserved.

No part of this book may be reproduced in any form or by any electronic or mechanical means, including information storage and retrieval systems, without written permission from the author, except for the use of brief quotations in a book review.

ALSO BY MICKEY MILLER

Blackwell After Dark - Small Town Romances

Sports Romances Series - Ballers

Playing Dirty

The Casanova Experience

Mickey Miller books cowritten with Holly Dodd:

Dirty CEO

Hotblooded Prizefighter

Subscribe here to my email list here so you don't miss out on any new releases! All of my releases are 99 cents for the first few days: http://eepurl.com/cjHaxD

SOUNDTRACK TO BOSS WITH BENEFITS

Just Friends - G-Eazy
Tequila Makes her Clothes Fall Off - Joe Nichols
Meant to be - Bebe Rexha and Florida Georgia Line
Motivation - Kelly Rowland and Lil Wayne
Hypnotize - Notorious B.I.G.
Mo Money Mo Problems - Notorious B.I.G. ft P. Diddy & Mase
Monster - Kanye West
Give Me Some of That - Thomas Rhett

CHAPTER 1

Sebastian

Some sons of bitches just don't know how to close a deal.

I'm not one of them.

I built Blackwell Industries from the ground up. They used to call me "The Finisher" as a matter of fact.

Even today, I'm in the middle of finishing someone else's business.

"Who the hell is holding up the Blackwell Ranch Proposal?" I bark loudly into my speakerphone.

"Someone named Brett Blue is the problem. Won't sell. Dad's land, that kind of thing."

I fume as I stare out the window of Blackwell's tallest building. When the first of the Blackwell linage arrived to this town years ago, their industry of choice was well-digging.

My business does *everything*.

"Completing the land sale is the key to this whole damn operation, John!"

"I know," he says nervously. "I just didn't close. I even offered the price you said."

"A half million. You offered the Blue family a half mil and they said no?"

"Didn't even flinch at the price," John answers.

"The Blue Estate isn't even worth two hundred thousand anymore."

"Brett Blue said, and I quote, 'That's not even in the ballpark of what I'll accept from Blackwell Industries, you rich pig.' End quote."

I furrow my brow. *Brett Blue*. Where do I remember that name from? I've met thousands of people over the years in the Blackwell area. Done business with hundreds of them. Didn't I know a Blue from back in the day? I rack my brain, but draw a blank.

"So this Brett Blue literally called me a 'pig?'" I growl, running my thumb and forefinger along my forehead.

"Spot on," he says, and I hear the sound of a car door slamming.

I rake a hand through my hair. *Why does that name sound so damn familiar?*

"Look John, we need this house to close or else the entire development for Blackwell Ranch is falling straight to shit. Do you understand that?" There's venom in my voice. John knows he failed. But he's my number one sales closer. If he couldn't get the job done, there's only one other option.

"Shit, you're right. I'll go back in and see what I can do."

"No, don't bother," I breathe, taking him off speaker. "I'll get it done myself."

"But Sebastian, I can handle-"

"If you could *handle* this, you would be driving back here

with the deed in your hands to the Blue property. Just…meet me there. I'll be there in half an hour."

"It's an hour away," John quips back.

"I know."

John's a nice guy. A good guy. He doesn't get that speed limits don't apply to me.

"Well alright then," is all he says.

I slam down the phone, grab my keys and sunglasses, and basically sprint out the door.

"Where to, Sir?" my secretary Fiona asks me as I rush out, tipping her head up toward me.

"Cancel all my appointments today. Something urgent came up and I need to take care of it."

"Of course, Sir."

Fiona smiles, flashing her bright white teeth at me as I head to the elevator and press the button to the parking garage.

I regard my reflection for a moment in the stainless steel of the elevator. I'm not going to lie, I'm a handsome dude. And I don't say that in a cocky way.

Well, actually, fuck that. I *do* say it in a cocky way.

My dad was a blue-collar hero to me—he ran a shop for thirty years before he finally retired to the farm. He didn't teach me much about the kind of business I run, but he did teach me the value of ironing your shirt and looking like a million bucks every day.

My suits are all custom tailored, like the dark navy blue one I'm wearing today, with a white shirt. The color contrasts nicely with my dark brown eyes.

Ever since I was born in Blackwell, almost thirty years ago, this town has never known what to do with me; they called me a 'big fish in a small pond.'

Whatever that means. I don't consider myself a fish, nor

do I shoot for small ponds. I aim to be the deadliest shark in the biggest ocean.

And Brett Blue, you just fucked with the Great White shark. This guy has no idea what's coming for him.

I don't lose deals. Not my thing.

The elevator hits the parking garage and I stride toward my personal spot, painted black. I turn my key in my Harley, pump the throttle a couple of times, and head out into the ebbing Blackwell summer.

Thirty-five minutes later, I roll up to the Blue Estate and put my motorcycle in park along their gravel driveway. I have to smile a little bit just looking at the place, as it's so classically homely. One side of the residence is lined with cornstalks as far as the eye can see, and the other side is a grove of apple trees. The main house in the middle is an old, colonial style build; big with two stories, and the house itself is an appropriate color given their family name: blue.

I walk toward John, who leans against his grey Honda Accord.

Even without my suit coat, I'm sweating just the slightest bit in the hot Blackwell summer sun.

"They know we're here?" I ask John as we shake hands.

"If they didn't before, they damn well do now. You can hear that motorcycle of yours for miles in all directions."

"Oh, right," I say, and rake a hand through my hair as I stare down the front door.

As I've built my fortune over the past decade, the element of surprise has come to be one of my favorite weapons. Usually it works in my favor, because most people have no idea what to make of me. Am I a suit? A country boy?

Nobody knows.

Hell, sometimes I don't even know myself. Although I'm

Blackwell born and bred, I have enough attitude that I tend to do just as well with those city sharks. Which is fine, because I have to deal with a lot of assholes in my line of work.

"So where's this Brett guy? He heard me roll up, and he's just gonna cower in the house all the same?" I scoff.

"Uh, Sebastian, Brett is a—"

"Clown who wouldn't know a good deal if it hit him in the face," I cut him off as we traipse together to the front door. "I know. I feel you. Sometimes it just takes the Boss's presence to help a man understand what a good deal he's getting."

John seems like he's got some other bullshit on the tip of his tongue—as usual, since he's a chatty sales type—but I'm not about to listen to any more of his excuses on this piece.

He lost the deal. Now I'm swooping in to close the deal. Simple as that.

Once we take the few steps up onto the porch, I reach for the old-fashioned knocker on the door, but before I do, the door swings open.

And a girl in a Blackwell University baseball cap answers.

She's so gorgeous, I have to fight to keep my jaw from dropping.

Strands of long blonde hair fall to her shoulders, her hair is a golden hue that nearly matches the yellow "B" of her hat. She's short—five feet tall maybe. And I can't stop staring.

"Hi, there," she says in a thick rural Blackwell accent. It's a little bit of southern, a little midwestern, and a lot of sweet and sexy sounding. "Can I help y'all?"

I swallow. Her eyes are a deep sea blue. She's got on denim short shorts, boots, and a white t-shirt. Dirty blonde hair falls just past her shoulders.

John says something like he's about to butt in, but I cut him off.

5

"Hello, Miss. I'm looking for Brett Blue. Is he available?"

I look over at John, and he's got a frightful expression on his pale face. Like all the blood has run out. He starts to say something, but I shoot him the look of death and he shuts his mouth.

The lovely lady cocks her head to the side a little and puts her hands on her hips, like she's amused. She turns her head a little, like she's going to call out the name to her household.

Behind her, going along the staircase, there's a shotgun hanging on the wall.

Damn. Doesn't get any more Blackwell than that.

With a devious smirk, she turns her head back toward me. "Hi. I'm Brett Blue. Now what can I help you with?"

My skin tingles and my heart flips. I flash a close-lipped smile.

I look her up and down, then turn to John.

"This is Brett?"

He shrugs. "Yeah. This is Brett."

I whip my glance back around, my eyes wide.

This girl is the one who's preventing me from completing my dominion west of Blackwell?

If she's two inches over five feet tall, I'd be surprised. She aims her chin toward me.

Her gorgeous chin.

"Can I help you?" she asks bitingly, raising an eyebrow.

"Yes ma'am," I say. "My name's Sebastian Blackwell. How are you today?"

I extend a hand, but she doesn't budge.

"I know who you are."

"Oh, good to hear. Would you mind if I come in? It's awfully hot outside."

I smile the same charming smile that helped me close my first deal, and every deal thereafter. She pauses and tosses her hair, not saying anything.

Even though she doesn't say anything, I move to step inside.

Rule number one of closing a deal: Assume the sale.

"Na ah ah," she says as she presses her palm against my chest, stopping me from entering. She's stronger than I thought she'd be. "I didn't say come in."

"But you didn't say no," I argue. "Where's your Blackwell hospitality, anyway?"

She chuckles a little, unflustered. "Now look here, Mr. Blackwell. Hospitality is something I give very freely. But not to men who want to come inside my house without even making their true intentions known. You want to buy this place. You want to close the deal that your little assistant couldn't."

I hesitate. This girl clearly has a no-bullshit tolerance. What else is a guy to do? I tell her the truth.

"Fine. You know why I'm here, so why don't I just put all my cards on the table. I want to buy this house. And this property. You've sold most of the acreage. Why not just finish it off?"

She holds her smile and cocks her head a little, her hair jostling to the side. "Let me ask you something. Do you see a 'For Sale' sign in front of the place?"

I take a deep breath. "No. But--"

"Glad you understand. My grandfather built it with his bare hands. It's staying in the family."

"How much did John here offer you?" I ask.

She keeps her lips locked tightly, and my heart starts to hammer.

I can't tell if it's because I might actually lose a deal for once, or because Brett Blue is the prettiest girl I've ever seen.

And there's just something about seeing her in her natural element, with a baseball cap, in boots and short shorts that has me thinking about things I should never consider with a client I'm buying from.

Or should I say *potential client*.

"How much?" I repeat.

"You know what, it doesn't matter. I wouldn't sell this place for a million bucks. Have a nice day you two. And don't come back. Else I might be forced to take that thing off the wall."

"What thing?" John butts in.

Brett smiles and shoots a glance behind her at the shotgun.

"Have a nice day, gentlemen."

She slams the door in my face.

CHAPTER 2

rett

I SHUT the door when the two men leave and take a deep breath. I lean against the door, my heart thumping like a tribal drum.

What the hell just happened?

Did I really just tell off the richest man in Blackwell?

I'm about to set my mug on the coffee table, but I hesitate when I see this year's edition of *Forbes* Thirty Under Thirty richest people list.

And guess who is on the cover?

Sebastian Blackwell, that cocky asshole.

He was expecting a man. He apparently didn't even remember me from my first job, years ago.

I sure as hell remember him.

I thumb through the magazine and read the blurb about him.

MICKEY MILLER

Sebastian Blackwell

The small town, homegrown businessman is famously known as the "Blue Collar Billionaire." Born into a poor family in the small town of Blackwell, he made his first million in his early twenties. After high school, with nothing but the work ethic his dad instilled in him and a one-way bus ticket, he moved to an oil boom town. In Louisiana, he worked eighteen-hour days of hard labor as a hand. He even claimed that for months at a time he would sleep on friends' couches or the streets to save every penny. After that, he moved back to his hometown and made a series of investments, each one more spectacular than the last, and was an early investor in cryptocurrencies. His net worth is estimated to be close to three billion.

So what are his next moves? Mr. Blackwell says he wants to take on an ambitious schedule of constructing both a world-class ranch and a distillery in the land around his hometown, Blackwell. He says it will bring jobs back to the area and restore the heartland.

I hear my mom's steps, as she traipses down the stairs. "Who was it, honey?" she asks, her voice raspy, as she's still waking up.

"No one," I croak. "Just some traveling salesman."

"A traveling salesman?" she asks as she gets to the bottom of the stairs. "What were they selling?"

"Rugs," I say quickly, the first thing that comes to mind.

"Rugs?" she parrots. "Well, we could use a good rug in the living room to tie the place together."

My mom's voice is soft and kind, but she still seems out of it.

She hasn't been the same since my dad passed away earlier this year.

Neither have I.

"But honey, you know we don't have the money for rugs. Oh dear me, you didn't buy one, did you?"

"No, Mom." I swallow. "I know that money's tight."

A woosh of butterflies overtake my stomach.

"We'll make it honey," she smiles warmly, and her optimism is contagious.

"I know," I say, and resign myself to the fact that the little thing that happened this morning will have to go into the category of 'what Mama doesn't know, doesn't hurt Mama.'

"But honey, there is something I need to tell you. Why don't we take a seat on the couch?"

"Alright. Would you like coffee? I made some already this morning."

"Of course."

I join my mother on the couch in our living room, and hand her the hot mug. Even in the dead of summer, she's always been the type of person who prefers her liquid hot.

"Honey, I've been meaning to share something with you. I should have told you months ago, but with everything that happened...I just couldn't find the right moment."

My face tightens, and worry pulses through me. The blood in my veins feels cold. My mom is rarely serious.

Much less when it's barely nine a.m. on a Tuesday.

"Your father, you know he had some debts after his treatment."

"Well yeah, of course."

Mama closes her eyes and nods. She tips her chin up and looks up toward the ceiling, like she's searching for something invisible.

She takes my hands in hers. "Since I didn't have enough to pay them a lump sum, I've been making monthly payments. The hospital has us on a payment plan for all of his treatments, but we still owe three thousand a month for the next two years. The longer we wait, the more we owe."

"Are you serious? That's bullshit! They can't do that!"

She nods, and a tear drop slowly heads down her cheek.

"They can, and they are doing it."

My jaw drops and my heart feels like it wants to jump out of my throat.

I take a deep breath. "It'll be okay, Mom."

She starts to cry outwardly. I join her.

All of a sudden, I have the worst feeling in the world.

I could have sold the place and our problems would have been solved.

The question remains in my mind, though.

Why does Sebastian Blackwell so badly want the Blue Estate?

It's only sixty acres. The man is so rich he could buy the moon if he wanted...

Right?

"So we won't be buying rugs any time soon," she says.

I nod. "I get it. No rugs any time soon. Now I'm gonna head out and get some work done."

LATER THAT DAY, after I've spent some time taking care of things on our farm and had dinner with my mother and little sister, I head up to my room.

It's interesting to be twenty-three years old and still living in your childhood room. There's something as comforting about it as there is confining.

After my father got sick, I had to drop out from my junior year in college to be at home with the family. It was just something I had to do, but now I'm a twenty-three-year old girl with two and half years of school and no degree.

And that doesn't get you much around here.

Come to think of it, nothing gets you much of a job

around here anymore. Ever since the Maytag plant that employed thousands of people moved its operations to Mexico, there really hasn't been much of anything here.

I chuckle to myself. Except, of course, Blackwell Industries. It's the only well-known employer for miles.

I sigh, realizing I've been staring at my computer screen and spacing out for a couple of minutes.

I refocus and do a Google search for 'jobs you can get without a college degree.'

That brings up a bunch of click-baity looking articles. I click on the first link, and unfortunately it requires that I move to Los Angeles.

I click the second. New York.

The third. Wisconsin.

I try my search again. This time, I put, *jobs you can get without a college degree in Blackwell.*

At the top of the page, there's an ad for Blackwell Industries. Curious, I click, and read.

Seeking: Sales Rep for West Blackwell Rep County. No degree required. Base salary 30k + incentives. Apply digitally by sending resume.

A glimmer of hope comes over me for a moment, and I wonder.

Could I make it as a sales rep?

No. That's silly. I'm a farm girl through and through. I could never do some stuffy sales job.

An ice-cold chill runs through my veins, as I remember how high and mighty I got this morning.

What on *Earth* was I thinking, telling Sebastian freaking Blackwell off like that?

Am I insane for what I did?

No. My father would be proud of me for sticking to my principles.

All the money in the world doesn't mean a man is happy, he used to say. *Money--that's just paper.*

Just paper indeed. But when you owe a few thousand a month, it sure feels a lot like indentured servitude.

Blackwell Industries has an easy as can be submission process. Since I already have my resume mostly ready, I tweak it and then hit submit.

I sigh. Somehow, I feel like I'll have to submit twenty resumes just to get one response back for an interview.

I click the 'back' button, and see what other queries my search result has brought up.

One article is interesting, but sorry, I won't be moving to an oil boomtown.

I click on another, for a maid in the local hotel.

Also a Blackwell Industries hotel job.

Shoot, I'm glad I didn't cave to that monster of a man, even if he offered me a ton of money. It's like he owns the entire freaking town.

I click and scroll to the second page of Google, always a clear sign of my desperation.

How am I going to even put a dent in my father's unpaid medical bills, and keep the credit collectors from coming after our house?

I see a curious headline, and I can't help but be intrigued.

How I Quit My Job and Became a Romance Writer.

It's some obscure blog that I've never heard of. There's not even a real name to go along with the site.

I glance to the shelf beside my bed, the one keeping my journals I used to write in every night.

When I click on the article, the author claims they were able to quit their full-time job at a restaurant and make almost as much money by writing romance novels.

Well hello.

I like writing.

And I like romance.

Why not give it a try?

What would I even write about?

Shoot, I haven't had any romance in my life since Patrick.

And as all my friends know, Patrick is the one who shall now never be named or brought up, after what he did to me.

Still, I read through the article, and I wonder if I could ever write a book some day. When I was nine, I wrote a bucket list. It had three things on it and was titled "My Three Goals in Life."

-Own a hot tub
-Eat lots of peaches
-Write a book

WHAT'S the worst that could happen if I at least tried to write something?

"Really, Brett?" I whisper. "You're going to write a bestselling romance novel? You haven't even been on a date in over a year. Where would you find your inspiration?"

With the stress of my dad being in the hospital for so long, I didn't have much time for a boyfriend. Plus, I always think about how my father always said no boy will be good enough for me. But thinking about the pickings lately in Blackwell, I have to say I agree. They are slim.

Still, I can come up with a story. I'm sure of it. I've got imagination for days.

I'm startled when my cell phone buzzes on my desk.

I pick it up. I don't recognize the number.

"Hello?"

"May I please speak with Miss Blue?" says a woman's voice on the other end.

"Speaking."

"My name is Fiona Marshall. I'm with Blackwell Industries. How are you this evening?"

My heart about jumps up through my neck. They're calling me back *already?*

"I'm well, and you?"

"Just fine. I'm going to cut to the chase. You applied for a position in sales at Blackwell Industries today, did you not?"

"Yes, I did," I say. *Barely a freaking half hour ago.*

"Excellent. Well, we'd like for you to come to our headquarters for an in-person interview."

I swallow. "Al-already?" I silently curse the fact that I just stuttered. *Confidence, Brett.*

"Yes. How is tomorrow at eight a.m.?"

I blink, and my vision drifts off to the street, where a sole black Lincoln Town Car is passing through the street. It looks out of place.

"I can do that," I say with feigned confidence.

"Excellent. I'll send the instructions to the email you used to submit the application. I realize this is a bit fast, but we just had a position open up and we're looking to fill it ASAP. I look forward to seeing you tomorrow, Miss Blue. Thanks, and have a nice--"

"Wait--one question," I manage to say quickly, before she hangs up.

"Yes?"

"Who will I be interviewing with?"

"With Mr. Blackwell."

A knot forms in my throat. "Okay, thank you. See you tomorrow."

I hang up.

In a daze, my eyes dart again to the shelf where I keep my journals.

My mind drifts to my first encounter with the man, one that apparently didn't even register very much with Sebastian.

I get up out of my chair and pull out one of them, dated seven years ago, when I was sixteen.

I'd hoped somewhere in my heart that Sebastian Blackwell, the cocky asshole, would remember me after all these years. I suppose I wasn't even a blip on his radar when we kissed all those years ago.

I thumb through my journal, finding the entry from July 4th, and read the short story I wrote from that day.

JULY 4TH -
"It was the best of times, it was the worst of times."
-Brett Blue.

Okay, allow me to explain that. I've been having an interesting time working at my new job. It's only my second week working at Blackwell Country Pizzeria, and today, I had the best and worst customers ever. I figured Mrs. Saracimi, my English teacher, would be proud of me for quoting A Tale of Two Cities. Now, without further ado, here is the story I wrote about the hottest man in Blackwell.

SEBASTIAN BLACKWELL, *who owns Blackwell Country Pizzeria, came in with his little brother Liam and I got to wait on them. He's looking more handsome than any man has a right to. I kept stealing glances at him as I passed by his table, and my heart raced every time our eyes connected. The best customer ever.*

Now, let's get to the worst.

A little later in the evening, a party of eight rolls in, and from the first moment I walk up to them, they are weirding me out, and I get the sense they're gonna be trouble.

They order four pizzas, all custom-built. I take detailed notes, double-check their order, and then punch their order into the POS system. I get double-sat right then, so I go and take orders and got drinks for those two tables. Well, about fifteen minutes later I go to check on their pizzas, since that's how long they typically take to cook normally.

Marcus, the cook, is confused when I ask him about the four custom-made pizzas.

"I've only gotten two pizza orders in the last twenty minutes. And they went out to table six on the patio already." Marcus check the receipts of the orders in front of him. "Yeah, I've got nothing." He shrugs.

A brick suddenly forms in my stomach. "Oh," I say.

"Did you put it in the system?" he asks condescendingly.

"Yes! I did!"

"Well you better double-check it." He shrugs. "I can't make a pizza if I don't have the order.

I race over to the nearest computer system to check on the order.

It's right there. I put it in seventeen minutes ago.

I run back to the kitchen, sweating bullets. I need to tell Marcus.

As I'm running across the restaurant, the guy who is at the head of the table grabs me by the elbow.

"Hey, lady! Where the hell are our pizzas? We've been waiting a while."

I take a deep breath, straighten my spine, and look him in the eye.

"Sir, I'm sorry. We had a kitchen error, and we're remaking the pizzas right now."

He sneers. "You're joking right?"

"I'm afraid not."

He rolls his eyes and mutters under his breath to the guy next to him. "Figures we get an airhead blonde for a server. It's like talking to a wall with her."

My chest swells, and I feel tears bubbling to the surface. "Excuse me?"

The guest chuckles, then looks me dead in the eyes. "Alright, well I might as well say it to your face. You're not the smartest server here, are you? You took an easy order, messed it up, and ruined our night because you are incompetent. It's pizza, lady, it's not rocket science."

I sniffle, holding back tears. I'm at the brink of crying, when I feel a hand on my shoulder.

It's the owner, Sebastian Blackwell.

He's the strong silent type, but when he speaks, the whole room listens. He just has this presence that has the ability to take over the room.

"What's the problem here, Sir?" he bellows, his voice deep.

"The problem," the guest sneers, "is that your server here doesn't know how to take an order. She has one job. Take the order. Write it down. Put it in the machine. It's so easy, a monkey could do it. But wait, I bet a monkey could do a better job of getting our order to us on time. We're fucking starving here."

My heart beats so hard, I think it might explode. Sebastian turns to me, and I'm wondering if he'll unleash on me for messing something up.

Instead, he turns back to the guest.

"I'm going to have to ask you to leave," Sebastian says calmly and authoritatively.

The man's face turns into a severe frown.

"The fuck you are," he scoffs. "We're getting our pizzas, and you're giving them to us for free."

Sebastian doesn't flinch in the slightest.

"I'll not tolerate that attitude, nor your verbal abuse of my employee. I'm going to say it nicely once more so I'm clear, Sir. Please leave. Now."

I see the man clenching his fist. Suddenly, he jumps to his feet, and takes a swing at Sebastian.

Sebastian sees the move coming, and he ducks like he's Keanu Reeves in The Matrix. *I put my hand over my heart.*

He then grabs the guest's arm and takes the man down to the ground and holds onto him, pressing his body against the floor.

A collective gasp goes up from the all guests in the restaurant.

"Sir," Sebastian says. "You've just committed assault. I'm going to hold you here while Brett calls the cops."

"I'm sorry." *The man can barely breathe.* "My father just died suddenly this week. We're all here after the funeral. It's got me on edge. I'm being an asshole. I'm sorry."

Sebastian's face softens at this news. He loosens his grip and lets the man up.

The guest looks at me. "I'm sorry I called you those things." *He shrugs.* "Been on edge all week. And I've been looking forward to that damn pizza."

"I'd better go check on my other guests," *is all I manage to say.*

I watch Sebastian from afar as he and the guest chat for twenty straight minutes. The pizzas arrive and the guest pays them no heed. Eventually they shake hands. Sebastian comes over to me.

"You're very smart, you know that, right?" *Sebastian says to me.*

"Yes?" *I answer in a question.*

"'Yes.' Say it like a statement. I watched the entire interaction from start to finish. The guest was just telling me that, all things considered you actually handled their table like a pro. So good job."

"You were...watching me?"

"I don't miss anything that happens in my restaurant." *He smiles slightly, tapping his head.* "You did good."

"You really think I did good?"

He nods, and I notice how Sebastian's long eyelashes are the perfect complement to his dark eyes. When I inhale, I can't help but take in a waft of his woodsy, masculine scent. I wonder if that's his cologne or his aftershave or what. Whatever it is, it's intoxicating.

My heart speeds up. I don't know exactly what I want from him, but I want...something.

Though I should definitely not be thinking about him like this.

He's six years my senior. Still, I can't help wondering what it would feel like to run my hands up and down his muscular arms.

Our eyes meet, and his linger on me.

I glance quickly around the restaurant to make sure there isn't anyone staring at us.

This is half premeditated, half impulsive, but I can't help myself. There's an opening and I go for it.

I lean in and kiss him on the lips.

My toes curl and butterflies flutter in my stomach. I've kissed boys before, but I've never been made to feel quite like this. It's electric, and my whole body shakes with desire for him.

He pushes me off lightly, and I swear I see reciprocating desire in his eyes too. But his words sadden me.

"Brett," he says softly. "What the hell are you doing?"

"I'm...thanking you," I mouth.

"You're great. You really are, but we can't do this. Please, you should find a guy your own age. And who's not the owner of this restaurant."

"Okay," I breathe.

MY HEART SPEEDS NOW, as I read the story I wrote about the cocky bastard, even though it was seven years ago. At sixteen, I crushed on him hard, like only a sixteen-year-old girl can. Yet today, he doesn't even know who I am. He's probably got plenty of girls crushing on him like this.

"Asshole," I mutter, closing my journal. I jump into my bed, on top of the covers.

Why is it that the assholes are always the hottest? It's like some inevitable law of nature that is totally unfair.

Even now, as I think about Sebastian, I can't help but skim my hand over the lace of my underwear a few times, then hover on the sensitive part.

I've always wondered what Sebastian would feel like on

top of me—if he'd be rough and in control, or the kind to drag out my pleasure until I just couldn't take any more. When he's in a suit, his pants pressed with a perfect crease down each thigh, he's the epitome of a man in control, a man who'd stop at nothing to get what he wants.

But without the tie, he's someone completely different. He's not your average over-the-top alpha male billionaire. He has this relaxed demeanor, like the country boy next door who can get down and dirty with the best of them. More casual, more layered than some suited businessman.

Still, he does look damn sexy in a suit.

My clit swells, throbbing with heat and need, begging for relief. I slip my hand beneath my panties, and the first soft, desperate moan escapes.

Why have I not gotten over him?

Sebastian's the type of guy who would seem to have unlimited patience until you crossed his line, and then he'd unleash on you.

I dig the fingernails of my free hand into the pillow above me.

I'd love for him to unleash on me.

My hips rock ever so slightly with each stroke of my finger.

As I touch myself, a scene unfolds in my mind, almost uncontrollably. I don't fight it, nor do I question what it means. I just give in and allow it. I visualize it and give the details free rein.

He enters my room, a country boy in a charcoal grey suit.
"Hello Brett. You're so wet thinking about me, aren't you?"
Yes. God yes.

He stares at me with his dark brown eyes, taking off his suit coat and tossing it onto the back of a chair. His frame is slim at the waist and wide at the shoulders.

"I've been thinking about this for years," he continues. *"Fuck,*

Brett, you look so damn sexy. When the hell did you grow into a woman?"

I rub my finger over my swollen clit and another moan escapes me, louder this time.

Still with a laser focus on me, he removes his tie.

Followed by his light blue collared shirt and undershirt, showcasing his beautifully toned body.

He takes it *all* off.

My breath hitches as he removes his pants, and his dick is as big as his presence.

He slowly strokes it as he walks toward me.

"I can't wait to be inside you, Brett. But first I want to do this."

Sebastian unhurriedly kisses each of my legs, starting at my calves, until he lands between my legs with his head.

"I've wanted to taste you for so long."

Softly, he tongues my clit, barely touching me.

I moan again.

Finally, he takes out his thick cock.

"Beg for it."

"Please."

"Please what?"

"Please fuck me."

He penetrates me slowly, inch by naughty inch. It's not long before he rocks into me with his whole weight.

Oh God.

I moan louder, and glance at the door to make sure it's closed.

Screw it. I throw my panties off and spread my legs. I'm so wet.

I press my fingers on my swollen nub, rubbing in a tight circle.

My other hand drifts to my breast and I pinch my nipple.

"Oh God," I mutter as I come, panting.

CHAPTER 3

Sebastian

It's an old rule of sales.

If you can't beat someone, *hire them*.

On the surface level, it might seem counterintuitive. But a hallmark of a good entrepreneur is knowing when and how to put your ego aside for the good of the company.

And yeah, I admit. I have a nice-sized one.

Ego, that is.

I know talent when I see it. And Brett Blue is the very definition of talent with a capital "T."

I smile as my eyes drift over Brett's resume. Somehow, she managed to stretch her twenty-three years of life, including just two and a half years of college, into one and a half pages of bullshit.

I have to hand it to her though, because she's got some decent writing skills to do so.

I peruse her very first bullet point.

Blackwell Country Pizzeria – Server – two years
 -Worked twenty hours/week in Blackwell's most bustling restaurant at the time
 -Ensured maximum satisfaction for patrons
 -Extensive knowledge of a menu featuring over eighty different items
 -Kept calm in the face of unruly customers

Holy shit. *That's* where I know her from.

I snap my fingers in realization.

In my early twenties, I was all in on starting the 'Blackwell restaurant renaissance' in this town.

Brett worked for one of my restaurants. "Tomboy" Blue is what the crew used to call her. She was just skin and bones back then. And having a name that was typically reserved for a guy made it easy for the kitchen staff to give her crap.

I reread the line she wrote, 'kept calm in the face of unruly customers.' My memory goes wild, and I remember one fourth of July when a customer got out of hand and tried to punch me.

And she went in for a kiss to thank me.

Brett Blue planted one right on me in a completely inappropriate fashion.

Damn if she hasn't come into her own since then. She's anything but a tomboy now, though the way she tried to hide her feminine beauty with that baseball cap showed shades of her past personality.

Fuck, she was hot when I saw her yesterday. Sea blue eyes, those hot lips, and blushing cheeks. I doubt she even had any makeup on.

Is getting a boner during a negotiation an acceptable reason to lose a deal?

No, fuck that.

Only soy-boys can't control their attraction. You know the type I'm talking about. The type of "men" who are more likely to be able to make a soy latte than to be able to do anything with their hands, or go hunting and actually come back with a kill.

Soy-boys.

Me?

I'm more comfortable on a tractor than in an air conditioned, sterile office. I live for the battlefield--which for me is one of snapping necks and cashing checks. And despite the affinity I've developed for my array of custom-made suits, I'd take a day on the lake fishing any day over the office.

There's a knock on the door, and before I can react at all, it opens.

I'm expecting to see Brett, the little shit. I don't doubt she would be the type of girl to knock on the door and not wait for me to tell her to enter, even on her very first interview.

But instead, in enters Blackwell Industries' in-house lawyer, Kim Murphy.

"Oh, hi there," I say, rising from my chair. "I wasn't expecting you."

Kim flashes her eyes as she comes toward me. Today she's got on lots of mascara that emphasizes her eyes, to go along with the power pantsuit she's wearing today.

Once at my desk, she shakes my hand with a wry smile. "Like you always said, surprise is one of the best weapons to have in your arsenal."

I cock my head and squint her way, examining her face to see if it reveals the true nature of her visit. "Last I checked you were working *for* me. Not against me."

She smiles. "Of course, of course. That's a figure of

speech. Now, I have a couple of updates for you. And Fiona told me you have an interview coming in today for the open sales role, so I thought I might sit in on it."

I sit back down in my chair, and motion with an open palm for Kim to take one of the seats in front of my desk.

"What updates?"

"I was reading through the details of your Shallowater Distillery proposal. I know you're waiting on my 'okay' before crews break ground on that one."

"And what did you find?"

"Not good. Even though most of the development is in the southeast corner of Blackwell County, surveyors found that one wing of the design falls in Furview County, which is dry."

"Fuck," I say, slamming my hand on the desk. "We can figure something out though, can't we?"

"Yeah, sure. We can…it's just going to involve redoing the entire architectural design. Could take months with all the details involved. We're thinking about an "L" shaped design."

I clench my fist and take a deep breath. "Alright."

"What about the Oro Valley deal? Did you snag the Blue Estate yesterday?" Kim says, and I wonder if she's already found out but is just looking to twist the knife. "Fiona said you went out there yourself. Must have been serious."

"No, I didn't get the property I needed," I say, my voice a low growl.

"Why not?" Kim arches an eyebrow at me.

"I've been busy. I'm probably hiring someone new."

"Oh, okay. What's his name?"

"Brett Blue. And it's not a--" My intercom buzzes, interrupting me before I can finish my thought. I push the button to listen to my secretary.

"What?"

"Sir," Fiona says. "Miss Blue is here."

"Great. Send her in."

Kim scrunches her face up at me. "Brett's a girl?"

The door opens, and she has her answer as Brett enters my office, her long blonde hair falling freely around her shoulders. She dons a blue dress that hugs her hips and falls to her knees. It's tight yet classy, and if I'm being honest, she looks stunning. A far cry from the farm girl with a baseball cap I met yesterday morning, though I found that version of her equally attractive, if not more so.

Shit, did I say attractive? Fuck that word. It's too soft.

She's downright mind-blowing.

Blowing...

Shit. My dirty mind takes off on its own, and suddenly I'm picturing Brett bobbing up and down on my cock in the office, me holding her blonde hair out of the way.

I scrub a hand on my chin and push all of those dirty thoughts to the closet of my mind and shut the door.

"Hi Mr. Blackwell," she says in a professional tone of voice, that lovely Blackwell accent sprouting from her tongue.

I clear my throat. "Miss Blue. You're right on time. Have a seat, please." I gesture with an open hand to the seat right next to Kim.

"Miss Blue, meet Miss Murphy. Miss Murphy has been Blackwell Industries' in-house law council for many years."

"So nice to make your acquaintance," Brett says with an outstretched hand. Kim seems a little reluctant, but she takes the hand and they shake.

I take a deep breath and Brett turns to me, batting her eyelashes, and again she catches me just slightly off guard.

Kim has a grim, fake looking smile on her face as she sits with her legs crossed and her posture a little too upright. I'm not sure what's got her panties in a bunch.

I refocus and fold my hands on my desk, forearms right on top of Brett's resume.

"Brett, let's not dance around why I've brought you in here. Strangely enough, after our encounter yesterday, you applied for the open position at Blackwell Industries. Why?"

"I need a job," she says without hesitation.

"So you turn down a lucrative offer for me to buy your property, then proceed to apply for a job that pays thirty thousand base salary? I'm just trying to understand your logic."

She raises her chin, her expression steady.

"My grandpa built our house with his bare hands. I'm not giving it up so you can build...whatever giant corporate operation it is that you're thinking of building on top of my family's property."

I nod. "I respect that, in a way. Even though I disagree with you. A Blackwell Industries Ranch would bring hundreds more jobs to the area. So why don't you tell us a little about yourself?"

She shifts, legs together.

"Well Sir, I'm born and raised just outside of Blackwell. I went to Blackwell High School, then took classes at the community college for two years. After that, I transferred to Blackwell U, but I ended up having to take a break from classes after a semester when my father got sick."

"I see. And you haven't thought about going back?"

"Of course I've thought about it. I just don't feel like going more into debt, when I already know what I want to do. I don't want to get some degree that ends in "studies" just so I can be in the same spot two years from now only with more debt."

I nod as I take a sip of my coffee, and I have to say I'm impressed. After spending all afternoon yesterday interviewing college graduates, there's no doubt in my mind she's whip-smart. Some of the kids that came in yesterday - shit. I felt like I was talking to high schoolers at best.

"What else would you like to know?" she asks.

"Well, you applied for this job and, quite frankly, you're much younger than every other applicant. Why did you apply for this job, specifically? Do you have an aptitude for sales?"

She touches her hair and flips it over her shoulder. "If you want the honest truth, I just googled 'jobs in Blackwell' or something like that and this one came up. I need a job. So I applied. It's that simple."

Kim nods, then stands up. "Well, thank you for letting me sit in on this interview for a bit. I just remembered I have a conference call I have to get to on the half hour," she says, and she heads toward the door. She pauses for a moment, looks at me, and then at Brett. "I'm sure the second half of the interview will go smoothly. Maybe you're just nervous because I'm here," she adds, her eyes small and squinty.

Brett laughs awkwardly. "I'm just getting warmed up." She winks.

"By the way, for your next interview, you probably want to take it easy on the perfume, Brianna," Kim adds.

"It's Brett. Like a boy's name, Brett," Brett repeats.

"Of course. Until next time." Kim cocks her head my way, smirking sly like we have a secret.

Which we don't.

Not really, at least.

I'm not sure what to make of Kim's snark.

I'm no expert in woman-speak, but I notice a bit of venom being exchanged between the two females, though I have no idea what it could be about. I mean shit, the two of them only just met each other.

I feel like I just saw a reenactment of a scene from *Mean Girls.*

I decide to stay focused at the task at hand, and turn my attention back to Brett.

Suddenly, I'm conscious of the fact that we are the only two in the room.

And she's running her tongue over her lips. She crosses her legs, shifts in her chair, and sets the gaze of her blue eyes on me, and I swear she must know some hypnotic techniques, because I'm mesmerized by her.

"Where were we?" I say.

"Oh, I think we were just getting to the part where you tell me whether or not I have the job." She smiles.

"Let's not get ahead of ourselves," I scoff.

"Well Sir," she returns. "I don't mean to be forward, but you called me literally thirty minutes after I applied. You brought me in for this interview lickity-split. I'm going to go ahead and assume you don't have much time to lose in getting your new hire on board. And that you haven't had much talent come in and apply for the position. I'm here, and I'm your talent. What else do you need to know? I'm an open book."

I lean back in my chair and shake my head, smirking ever so slightly. I can't believe this woman. First, she makes a fool out of my offer yesterday. And now, here she is pretending like she's already got the job when we're barely fifteen minutes into the interview.

She's already assuming the damn sale.

Shit, apparently she doesn't even have to read the book. She's a natural at negotiating.

And I'd be an idiot not to hire her.

Still, I'm not about to give her the job like it's nothing. I'll think of something good to challenge her with.

"Let's change gears for a moment, Brett. Do you have any questions about the position?"

"What will I be selling?" she asks. "And what's the day-to-day like?"

"Day-to-day, you're in the office, following up on a few emails, making calls, and making sure all of the purchases are in accordance with the local laws, that kind of thing. And also handling any special projects that may come along."

"And when I'm not in the office?"

"You'll be out in the field, getting people to sell their property to you. Since my plan to start a ranch east of Blackwell fell through, now I've got to try and build it west of Blackwell."

"Why did it fall through?"

"You really want to rub it in, don't you?"

"Rub what in?"

I can't tell if she's playing dumb, or is too naïve to realize what she did to me.

"Well I offered this family—the Blue family—a hefty sum for their rural estate to the east, but they turned me down. Without that central property, the ranch I'm planning to build will never work. So now I need to start buying up property to the west of Blackwell. And that's what I need you for. So you're not really selling a product—you'll be selling people—mostly gentlemen—on the idea of me buying their property…"

"So you can build a big ranch."

"Yes."

She falls silent and takes a deep breath.

"I'm a little conflicted, but alright. I guess I'll take it."

I laugh out loud. "You'll what?"

"I said I'll take the job."

"I haven't offered you anything yet."

"Oh, so I don't have the job? Well, I suppose I can see myself out then."

She stands abruptly, and heads for the exit.

"I didn't say that," I backtrack. She doesn't stop walking toward the door, her heels clicking on the hardwood.

Fuck. She *is* a master negotiator. And it's all instinct.

She's impressive.

I whip out from behind my desk, walk briskly to the door, and block her from leaving.

"I'm gonna hire you. Right here, right now. You report to work tomorrow at eight a.m. I'll have Fiona send you over the introductory packet and get the signatures and the paperwork taken care of. Got it?"

She looks me in the eye, then looks away at the door. "Yes sir."

"I'll have Fiona contact you with the details. See you tomorrow."

Motherfucker. Having a bombshell like her around the office is going to be an exercise in self-control.

But then, I have the most self-control of any guy I know.

I can do this, no problem.

CHAPTER 4

rett

To celebrate my new job, I meet up with my friend, Crystal, for drinks at our favorite local bar, The Watering Hole.

Her jaw drops as I recount how I got hired at Blackwell Industries.

"Let me get this straight. You told him off, and he *hired* you?"

"Yeah." I shrug. "It makes no sense to me either."

"You know what else makes no sense? How a billionaire could be that hot."

I nearly spit out my drink. "You're talking about Sebastian?"

"Oh please." Crystal rolls her eyes. "Don't act like you've been living under a rock. Here."

She pulls out her phone, pulls up the Instagram app, and shows me a picture.

"See? Look at those abs."

I take her phone and swallow. The photo is from a year or so ago, and he's with a woman who looks like if you looked up the word 'sexy as hell' in the dictionary, you'd find her picture. She's got a perfectly proportioned body. Sebastian compliments her well. If you looked up 'tall dark and handsome' you'd probably find his picture. His eyes are mocha-colored, and his body is wet in the picture. He's got a slight happy trail and a few hairs on his chest, but that doesn't take away from his six pack abs.

"That's...him? Holy shit." I swallow. "I only saw him in a suit. He's going to be the perfect muse for my romance novel."

"Um, what?" Crystal does a double take as I stare longingly at his picture, still puzzled over why the man chose to hire a girl like me. My skin flushes, and I wonder what it would feel like to run my hand along those abs. "Did you just say romance novel? You're going to have to explain that one to me."

I nod, but I'm in some sort of a trance looking at Sebastian's toned body.

"Stare much?" Crystal jokes. "I mean, you'll have plenty of time to stare at work. In person. Right?"

I shake my head.

"Dick!" I blurt out, my blood suddenly boiling as I remember how he tried to get me to sell my family property the other day.

"Dick?" Crystal takes her phone and examines the photo more closely.

I take a swig of my drink, still remembering how much of an uncaring asshole he seemed yesterday.

"Hmm," she says. "Yeah, now that you mention it, I think I can see the outline of his...you know...in that swimsuit. Wow."

"Crystal! I meant, 'he's a dick!' Not 'look at his dick!'" I throw my head back in laughter.

Crystal shrugs and puts her phone away. "Well apparently you are tongue-tied when talking about him. Understandably."

"But it's true. He's an asshole."

"So you're saying you wouldn't sleep with him?"

"You know my rule."

Crystal rolls her eyes. "No more assholes after Patrick," she says, imitating my voice.

"You mean after the one of whom we shall no longer speak of. Besides, this guy is dating models. It's such a ridiculous hypothetical question. It would never come up. Obviously, he likes willowy model types. I'm a curvy little blonde."

Crystal trails off and bites her lip. "Speak of the devil. The man enters like he's God's gift to women. Sad thing is, I can't say I blame him."

I turn my head to the front door and watch. To say Sebastian 'walks' in is not accurate.

He struts.

He's wearing jeans, a blazer, and has these boots on that are somehow as stylish as they are rugged looking. He looks like he could crossover from an office meeting as easily as he could head out into the cornfields and jump on a tractor.

"I wouldn't mind seeing him with his shirt off, heading into the fields for some hard labor," Crystal jokes, and I chuckle.

Inside, Sebastian is barraged by an array of service staff, asking if he needs anything, making sure the owner of the place and the one who pays their salaries is taken care of.

Figures--he's a hotshot.

The hostess leads him toward a booth in the corner.

As he walks past us, I realize something I didn't in the

office today, or when he came out to my place the morning before.

His shoulders are broad enough that I wonder why he didn't just become a professional athlete instead of Blackwell's most notorious deal-maker. Sure, maybe his blazer makes them a little broader, but not by much. And maybe it's the dim bar-light, but the way his dark features come out has me wondering and reinforces that I've found some romantic inspiration for my book that I have yet to start writing.

He looks in my direction and he must see me, though he doesn't even make eye contact with me. I certainly catch a whiff of his cologne as he walks by. It smells like the woods mixed with fresh mint.

Crystal sniffs the air. "Smells like Hugo Boss."

"What a dick," I mutter under my breath.

So he hires me in the morning, but outside of work he won't even say hi to me?

He passes me and he's already heading to a booth in the back of the bar.

"Um." Crystal coughs, turning her head back toward me. "Isn't he your new boss? He didn't even acknowledge your existence."

"No. He didn't."

"Maybe he didn't see you?"

"We're in the first two seats at the bar. How could he miss us?"

"I don't know." She shrugs. "Why don't you find out?"

"Find out how?"

"Go talk to him. I mean he looks lonely, sitting in the corner booth like that, doesn't he?"

"I guess he does."

She shrugs. "Just go ask him. I'll get us a couple of new drinks. Sound good?"

"Alright."

I watch as the bartender comes back from talking to Sebastian, presumably to take his order.

"Hey Mason?" I ask as he muddles the drink.

"What's up?"

"You mind if I bring that drink over to the gentleman in the corner?"

"You want to bring Sebastian Blackwell his drink? Why?"

"Because he's my new boss. And he's a dick."

CHAPTER 5

Sebastian

EVEN THOUGH I own all of the bars in Blackwell except for one, I don't even drink that much myself anymore.

Mason, the bartender, comes up from behind the bar and approaches the booth where I'm sitting solo with my convertible tablet-laptop and some papers spread across the table. "Mr. Blackwell." He nods, setting a water in front of me. "Surprised to see you in here on a weekday. But what can I get you, Sir?"

Mason is one of my little brother Liam's buddies. I like the fact that he knows how to address his superiors with respect. He's got that right combination of knowing how and when to be entertaining, and when to be serious and draw the line. It's an important skill to have when you're the head bartender at a place like The Watering Hole.

"I'll have an Old Fashioned with Bulleit Rye."

Mason smirks a little bit. "Same as usual. Sir, yes sir," he says, and heads back behind the bar to make my drink.

I lean back in my booth and take inventory of the place. There's a nice crowd tonight, especially for a Wednesday, which is typically one of the slower days in the restaurant business. It helps that tonight is a gorgeous September night, one of those where the warmth of the summer meets the cool of the incoming fall, and the temperature is so perfect you feel like you're in Florida in the winter.

On the bar stools, I notice a couple of hotties chatting, and the brunette seems to have her gaze slightly turned to me.

Her friend, whose image I can't quite make out from my spot in the back booth, is a stunning blonde in the shadows of this dimly lit interior.

After a fleeting glance at them, I focus my eyes back on the task at hand. I came here to run the big numbers over an Old Fashioned, not talk to girls. A younger version of me would have been on those two like white on rice.

I put my head down, open my tablet, and run through the architectural plans for the distillery which now have to be totally and completely overhauled because of a stupid oversight.

How did we not realize three acres of these plans were on the neighboring dry county?

It was quite the blunder by my entire architectural staff, to miss a detail like that so completely.

On the other hand, some college grads have trouble seeing the bigger picture. They're so focused on their papers and charts and equations and essays. They never think to take a step back and just ask some basic questions, like *what are the laws of the local jurisdictions in accordance to what we are building?*

They've got zero street smarts.

Much the opposite of a certain hire I just made this morning.

Brett fucking Blue. I look at the painting on the wall next to my booth and space out a little bit as I think of how much of an outlier this girl is. It's one of those 1960s Roy Lichtenstein dot paintings with attractive women.

Speaking of attractive women...Brett is incredibly sexy.

And smart.

And she even knows how to drive a tractor, and that sweet Blackwell accent of hers combined with that light voice has me hard just *thinking* about her.

I take a swig of my water and think for a moment, reminding myself how I can't be having these sorts of thoughts about employees. Especially when it's not even her first day. Sebastian Blackwell is one of the few rich men in the town who got that way by helping the town, not screwing people over.

And he definitely doesn't screw his employees. That is some small town drama that I definitely don't need.

I hear someone clear their throat, and a drink clunks on the wooden table. I turn to thank the bartender, and see if his drink-making skills are still up to par.

But when I look over, it's not Mason at all.

It's Brett Blue.

My adrenaline spikes like I'm a wild lion and an intruder has entered my kingdom. Her scent wafts into me, smelling like freshness and sunflowers and youth.

And she looks so smoking hot, that slight boner twitch I was joking about? Yeah, I've got to fight not to have a full-on salute going under the table right now.

She clears her throat and does what is quickly becoming her signature move, the slight head tilt. "The bartender wanted me to bring you this." She smiles.

"So you're moonlighting as a server now, too?" I remark. "You really are a sales personality by nature. You're a hustler."

"And you're a dick. You don't even say hello to me."

"I didn't even see you. I've got a lot on my mind right now. It's nothing personal."

She frowns. "Really. So I must not register very much on your radar. Even after you hired me."

I take a big breath through my nose. "So you think I'm a big asshole."

"Yeah," she says. "Pretty much. And I don't work for assholes."

I tilt my head and exhale.

"Fair enough. How about this? I interviewed you, today. Now is your turn to interview me. Ask me whatever you want. I'll respond honestly."

"Seriously. Anything?"

I take a sip of my Old Fashioned, it's delicious. The bartender arrives with another and sets it in front of Brett.

"I'll give you one drink. You're not even officially working for me yet, so nothing's off-limits. Starting now. Cheers."

We clink glasses, and each take a sip, keeping eye contact.

"Where were you born?" she asks.

"Blackwell."

"Your parents. Together or divorced?"

"Together. You?"

"My father passed away this year."

"I'm sorry to hear that," I say.

"Thanks. Where do yours live now?"

"They own a little small farm north of Blackwell."

"You get out there much?"

"I don't. Haven't been there for years."

"Why not?"

I shrug, and take another strong pull on my drink. "My father and I don't speak much. He respects my work ethic, but that's it. In a lot of ways, I think he blames me for the ruin of this town, and it's my fault people are struggling. Says I'm a mean businessman."

"What do you say to that?"

"I say he doesn't understand me. If anything, I've kept this town going."

She nods, and takes a sip of her drink. "So what doesn't he understand? Please, enlighten me, Bossman."

My fists clench on top of the table. She sees my tension. This isn't a topic I spend a lot of time explaining, but right now I've got no other option.

"Ten years ago, you remember what happened?"

"I was thirteen," she quips. "I don't know…I decided that I wasn't going to play softball in the summer because my parents said metal bats were too expensive?"

"No, but close. The Maytag…oh wait a second. Your mother, her name is Laura Blue, isn't it?"

She looks surprised. "How did you know?"

"She used to work at the Maytag plant with my mother. Before it closed down. *That* is what happened ten years ago. The plant took almost ten thousand jobs with it. Addiction and desperation spiked, and this town was headed for disaster."

"So what's that got to do with anything?" she scoffs.

I purse my lips and shake my head ever so slightly. "You are young, aren't you? You think you know about everything. But really, you've got a lot to learn. Do you know what I did with that first million?"

"Hookers? Bought a mansion? A yacht? I don't know."

My grip on my drink tightens. Funny, she's asking me for my life's story and though she's angry, she's riveted, her eyes wide as she leans forward on the table. I take a swallow of whisky, and fuck, her cleavage is in my peripheral vision now as she leans over. She's licking her lips. *Tempting* me.

Luckily self-control is one of my best assets, so I'm able to keep my eyes laser focused on hers as I continue my story.

"I invested half in Cryptocurrencies. Bitcoin, ethereum, and a few others. I did a lot of research, and I had a hunch they were going to blow up, and they have. The other half, I poured into development in the city of Blackwell. If this place was going to go downhill, damned if I was going to sit by idly and watch it burn. I was born here, and I'll damn well die here turning this place around. In my early twenties, I thought the restaurant business was how I was going to make my money. But then I learned that restaurant margins are paper thin. And also, a town that only has restaurants is doomed to fail. So I started looking for other places to invest and revitalize the town."

She puts the glass to her lips, and I take pleasure in watching every slow, sensual movement she makes. She looks at the painting on the wall in our booth as she mentally processes the truth bomb I just dropped on her.

"But you're an owner. You're an asshole. That's what everyone says. You're just a rich dickhead who doesn't give a crap about anyone's feelings. Everyone knows that. Haven't you seen the latest meme on Twitter about you?"

I lean into the table, and a smile broaches my face. "And did you just say Twitter? Fuck Twitter. And fuck Facebook too. I don't have time for that."

"That's a really dick-ish thing to say," she adds.

"Yeah? Well it's the truth."

Brett tosses her hair over her shoulder, and the corners of her mouth curve upward, ever so slightly. "So Mr. Blackwell," she says, finally a hint of sympathy in her voice. "You didn't even go to college, did you?"

"No," I growl. "Parents couldn't afford it. And after I'd already started making my own money, I saw no reason to go to college or any formal schooling for that matter."

"Wow," she says, nodding blankly. "I didn't...I wouldn't have expected that."

"Not a lot of people do. Most figure I was born with the silver spoon."

I finish the last of my drink, and we sit there in silence a moment. There's something about this girl that really gets me going. It's her fire. It's her curiosity. It's how she won't take anything at face value, and has to find out for herself.

It's the fact that she's hot as hell. She's got a black tank top and tight jeans on, and her breasts are busting out of her top. But moreover, her smile and her facial features are to die for. And inside, she's got this wonderful brain. She may be young, but she's very intelligent.

"Now I'm not saying I'm not a total asshole in individual dealings. But when it comes to the well-being of this town, if you ever question me again, I will not be very happy. I was born in Blackwell. I'll make my bread in Blackwell. And I'll die here."

A smile crosses her face. "Did you just paraphrase the lyrics to "Small Town" by John Mellencamp?"

"Nah." I wink. "I'd never do that. I'm more of a John Prine guy anyway."

She gasps. "You...know who John Prine is?"

"Peaches are the key to happiness," I say, and I don't show it, but I'm more surprised that *she* knows who my favorite obscure folk artist is. "So do we have a deal?"

She hesitates just as the song changes, and all the people in the bar come into focus. Finally, "Summer of 69" by Bryan Adams starts up on the jukebox, taking everyone off edge.

"Fine," she says, returning my shake. "I'm excited about the job. But not for the reasons you think."

I raise an eyebrow. "What do you mean by that?"

"Oh, uhh...I just mean, I-I," she stutters. "I'm going to

learn a lot. About sales. What are you working on right now, for example?"

She turns her head sideways to attempt to view what I'm working on.

"Have you heard about the Shallowater Distillery development?"

"I read the local newspaper. How could I miss it? It's supposed to bring in over three hundred new jobs to the area."

"Right. But the problem is, we can't move forward with it. I don't have enough room for the design we planned since part of our master plan falls on a dry county. The architects are scrambling to figure out how to make it happen. I needed to have this development operating by next summer. Lost plans mean time, and lost time means lost money."

"So why don't you just make it smaller?"

I rub my thumb and forefinger on my forehead. "I guess I *could* make it smaller, but then when it comes to production we're going to be hamstrung. There's a ton of demand in the area, and I need to make sure we can handle it."

"Can I see the design?"

"Uh, have you ever designed anything?"

She shrugs. "When I was younger, I helped my father build our barn. I had to measure out the sizes of the partitions for the chicken coops and the pigs, and the rest of the storage." She jingles the ice in her glass and flips her hair. "He called me his 'little designer assistant.'"

"Aww, well that's sweet," I say, spinning my tablet around so she can see the screen. "It's a professionally drafted design. It's probably a little hard to understand."

The words come out a little condescending, even though I don't mean them like that. But there's a big difference between an architectural draft and a barn on the farm.

She stares at the screen for a few moments. "Huh," she exclaims, nodding thoughtfully.

"Huh, what?"

She looks back at me, her blue eyes intense against mine. "This is just one floor?"

"Well, yeah. It's a one floor design almost all the way around. That's pretty standard for a distillery."

"Well why can't you make it two floors?"

I look at her, and for a moment it's like she's one of those little kids, asking "Why" a thousand times.

But she's got a point.

"I, I don't know. I just go with the design that my architects give me. I'm an entrepreneur, not a building expert. You've got a damn good point though. I'll check on that."

"I'll take my first commission in the form of fifty percent of the money you've saved from using my idea." She winks.

"How about I just buy a drink to celebrate?"

"What are we celebrating?"

"The fact that you just solved the problem I was going to be working on for the rest of the night. Oh, and you starting work tomorrow at Blackwell Industries, of course."

I order one more, and I can't take my eyes off her. Though I'm wondering what's behind those pretty blues. It's obvious to me she's much more than just a pretty face.

And I intend to find out what makes Brett Blue tick.

CHAPTER 6

rett

"Thanks for the ride today," I say to Crystal as I get into her car. Luckily, she lives even farther away from Blackwell than I do, and starts work earlier than me, so she's the perfect candidate to give me a ride to work today, since my Mom needed the car this morning.

And I'll be early to work by a solid hour, since I'm only normally supposed to be there by eight.

As I close the door, she turns the music down.

"Blasting Thomas Rhett already, eh?"

"Aw, it's never too early for a little bit of Tommy boy," she says. "But I never got the chance to ask you how the rest of the night went."

"Oh, it went fine. Sorry for ditching you. I…didn't know I was going to be talking to him for so long. But he brought me in and once he did, I felt like I was…under his spell or something."

"Yeah, I thought you were just going to tell him off."

"Well, I gave him some space to explain himself. And I don't know, maybe he's not as big of an asshole as some people say he is."

"No. Brett, just no. He's a big, giant villain. Everyone knows that. He's heartless. I heard he once fired someone just because they were five minutes late to their shift. He's horrible."

I recoil a little bit. "I haven't heard that."

"Just…be careful, okay? Although, just because he's not an asshole doesn't mean he's not hot." Her eyes get a little glazed over as she looks into the distance down my road, County Road D. "Speaking of hot, did you make any progress in finding inspiration for your book yet? Or are you still going to stick with…you know. Your potential boss?"

Pangs of nervous sweat begin to overtake me. "I think I'm going to stick with him. I wrote a chapter when I got home last night."

Her jaw hangs open. "A whole chapter! What's it about?"

"Uh," I stumble. I can't tell her who I was really fantasizing about last night. Can I? "It's really silly. But…What you said about Sebastian got me thinking. He *is* really hot. And he *is* a pretty big asshole. But I think that's a combination I want to write about. So I didn't think of him, exactly. Just someone who is *like* him. Like a prototype."

She nods, eyes still forward as she eats up the country road in front of us.

"I'm thinking of calling it…" I pause dramatically and move my hands across the window like I'm spelling out the words on a sign "My Hot Restaurant Boss."

With her lips parted, she looks over at me with crazy eyes. "Are you sure? That sounds like, really specific."

"Watch out!" I yell, and help her swerve at the last second to barely miss a cow drifting into the middle of the road.

She shrieks, but luckily since there are no other cars in the road, it's fine when we veer off into the oncoming traffic lane.

"Phew," she says as she slows and steadies the car. "You're distracting me with this ridiculous title! My Hot Boss at the Restaurant? Really? It sounds like the restaurant is hot, not the boss. And it's also just...I don't know. I think you can do better than that."

We pull past the city limits of Blackwell, and the tallest building comes into view.

Finally we pull up in front of the Blackwell Industries building. I pop out the door.

"Have a good first day at school, honey." Crystal waves. "Pick you up at four?"

"Yes, I think so. I'll text you."

I check my phone for the time. It's still early, not even seven a.m. yet. My father, rest his heart in peace, was the one who taught me that if you're early, you're on time, if you're on time, you're late, and if you're late, don't bother showing up.

And especially on a day like today, I'm excited I'm early. I go to *Daily Grind,* Blackwell's local coffee shop, and pick up a latté.

When I get to the Blackwell building, I realize it's been awhile since I woke up with adrenaline pumping through my veins as I enter the lobby.

"Hi," I say to the gentleman at the front desk. "My name is Brett. It's my first day."

"Ah, Brett Blue." He smiles. "I have your temporary ID right here. For now, take the elevator on the west wing on up to the seventeenth floor. Mr. Blackwell himself said he's going to be going through your orientation today. Just head on up."

As I step into the elevator and press the button for the seventeenth floor, I can feel my heart rate elevating.

I can say it's because it's the first day of a new job.

Or because I'm in the biggest building in Blackwell.

I'm stepping into Sebastian's lair.

I'm *not* attracted to him.

I swear.

But as I ride up in the elevator, I think I can detect that manly, woodsy scent of his. It probably permeates the whole place twenty-four hours a day seven days a week.

The elevator doors open, but floor seventeen is basically bare. I see a janitor walking around, but other than that, there's no one.

I walk past the opening to Sebastian's office, the door is closed and the lights are dark. I wonder if he gets here early, too. The guy does seem like the workaholic type.

I turn right and pass through the archway to the main cubicles. The lights are dimly lit, though the morning sun is shining in and visibility is no problem.

Weird. When I cleared everything with Fiona yesterday, she said someone would be here to meet me between seven and eight, but there's not a peep.

I head back to Sebastian's office, and figure I'll wait for him there. But now the door is cracked open just a smidge, and I can hear a strange noise coming from inside. It sounds like forced grunting.

"Oh yeah," I hear the voice say, unmistakably his. "Just like that," he says in a low murmur.

Holy shit.

Is someone...is he...having sex?

It's the first day on the job, and I'm already about to catch my boss hooking up with someone.

I know I probably should just mind my own business

based on the noise, and that there are some things the mind can't unsee. But I don't care. Like Tom Petty, I *need to know*.

After all the things Sebastian said yesterday to me, I was starting to think maybe he wasn't so bad of a guy. But if he's hooking up with like, one of the interns? Ew. Just no.

I set my latté on the secretary's desk, and get on my hands and knees so I'm low to the ground. I push the door open ever so slightly, just enough so that I'm able to get my tiny head halfway into the doorframe into an angle that makes me able to see the source of the noise.

I prepare myself for the worst. He's probably got the secretary facing the glass window of the wall overlooking the sunrise. And you know, I can't say I blame her for wanting a little bit of Sebastian early in the morning.

But when I look in, I don't see him hooking up with anyone. Instead, he's doing the most boring thing I've ever seen a man do:

Pushups.

To be fair, he's got his shirt off. After finishing one set, he jumps up to a pull up bar that is apparently installed on his wall.

"Oh yeah. Fuck yeah," he growls as he reaches the top of a rep.

Animal.

The man is a total animal. And I'm completely mesmerized by it. Maybe it's his six pack. Maybe it's his ginormous arm muscles. Maybe it's the way his manly musk fills my nostrils, and the fact that I can sense how much this man is half billionaire tycoon, half country boy.

But suddenly, at seven fifteen a.m. in the morning, on my hands and knees, I am getting worked up.

"Uh, Miss Blue?" someone says behind me, and I recognize Fiona's voice. Instantly, I knock my head into the doorframe, jarring it and my head. I jump up to my feet, but I'm off-kilter due to the hit I just took on the doorknob.

I resist muttering in pain.

Fiona doesn't have to say a word. She's wondering what the hell I am doing looking into my boss's office. And I don't blame her for being curious.

I think fast.

"I was just...looking for the cross on my cross necklace!" I say cheerily to Fiona. She looks back at me with curiosity. "Found it! And I already even reattached it to my necklace." I hold up my necklace as proof.

Darn. Did I just lie? I hate lying. Now I know this is only a little white lie, but I don't like those all the same.

My hand shakes as I go to grab my coffee, mustering a smile to flash at Fiona as she sits in her chair. I pick up my hot coffee and hold it in front of my chest, hoping it will steady me.

"Well, that's a nice necklace," Fiona says, her eyes examining me. "I'm glad you found it."

I clam up. Shoot. I don't think I've told a lie since high school. My nervousness makes my hands shake.

"Oh, I uh. Yeah. It's hot out today."

"Yes it is," Fiona says calmly as she fires up her computer. "Hot for early September. Not as hot as August though."

"Yeah--"

I don't know where I am going with my sentence, but my hands--for no apparent reason--think I'm holding butter sandwiches and my latté spills right out onto my chest and my white blouse.

"Ahhh!" I scream, and the heat seeps slightly into my skin. "Oh my God. Oh my God."

"Oh my God!" Fiona returns imitating me. She jumps up out of her chair. "Are you okay?"

"So hot!" I yell. I set my cup down and frantically try to whip off my blouse.

"What the hell--" booms a deep voice.

"Uff!" I utter as I run into what feels like a brick wall.

Of flesh. A brick wall of flesh.

Oh my God. My heart stops as reality hits me.

I just bumped into my boss, shirtless and with my hands lifted over my head.

Wearing only my bra.

"For the love of God, get in here," Sebastian says, ushering me into his office. He helps me pull the shirt off, and then it's as if he realizes the implications of what just happened, when he sees me in just a bra.

"I have an extra shirt." He turns abruptly, heads to a closet in his room, and pulls down a blue button down.

My heart hammers against my chest, because this man is gorgeous in person. I stare at his six pack abs and the rest of his muscled body up close.

"Put this on for now," he says. "I'll have someone go out and get you a new shirt soon. Okay?"

I blink. "Do you...always work out shirtless in the morning?"

"Yes of course. It's part of my office wellness routine." He licks his lips, and our eyes linger together for just a little too long. He grabs his shirt, which is draped over his chair, and starts to button it.

"How about another coffee?" Sebastian asks me, putting his hand on my arm. "How do you take yours?"

"I had a vanilla latté."

"Alright. I'll tell Fiona."

He buzzes Fiona through the intercom and tells her my coffee order.

"So," I say as I reach the top button of my shirt and tuck it in. I'm going to look ridiculous in this, but I suppose it's better than being naked. "You enjoyed the peep show?"

He buttons the top button of his collar, and begins to tie his tie.

"I should ask you the same question." He winks, and leans in. "Looking for a cross my ass. Don't pull your little white lies around here. Remember our little run-in in the restaurant? I see *everything*."

A current of electricity runs through my body.

"Sorry. I didn't mean to spy on you. I didn't think you would be here so early," I groan, thinking of ways to change the subject. "Hey, I don't look too ridiculous in this thing, do I?" I do a 360-degree spin in his huge shirt.

"You wear it well," he says, then clears his throat. "We'll just spend this first week getting the hang of things. Maybe we'll save the field visits for next week."

Anxious as I am to get started, he's got a point.

Finally, I leave his office, and minutes later Fiona shows up with another coffee. She leads me to my desk, which is in the middle of the floor between a couple of other cubicles. I'm flanked by a middle-aged man whose name is Ted, and a girl, Jackie, who appears to be in her mid-twenties.

"I've got to scoot," Fiona says after introductions. "Plenty of work to be done this morning. You remember Kim Murphy, right? She'll be giving you your full orientation this afternoon."

"Uh, so what should I work on until she gets here?"

"You could do some proactive research on the properties to the west of Blackwell. And I'm sure he'll have some more for you to do, soon. Mr. B's got a full schedule this morning though."

"You can do some of my work!" Jackie says chirpily with a wink.

Fiona walks away, and I get started on my first day.

I do a little research on the properties west of Blackwell, and find out what I had already suspected. Most owners are small farmers with a few residences mixed in as well. I recognize most of the names of the families with ownership. These are people who have been a part of the community for years.

My coworkers seem hard at work, but I have nothing to do. I glance over at Ted, and he's rubbing his face in what appears to be maximum frustration.

Barely an hour into the morning, and I'm already bored.

A devilish idea hits me, and immediately, I dismiss it because it's that bad. But the little voice keeps speaking in my ear.

Brett, why don't you just write a romance novel right now, at work?

It's a fair point. I don't have much else better to do at the moment.

I wonder if Blackwell Industries is the kind of company that has software on our computers for tracking what we do.

Nah, I doubt it. It's too much of a down home place. I decide I'll just pull up google docs in a browser so I can save it to the cloud and not to my work desktop. If anyone asks me, well, I'll just tell them I was sending a personal note to a friend.

A very dirty personal note.

I open the document and start writing chapter two of my story, which, incidentally, involves a boss, his young employee, and a coffee incident.

The words flow freely.

I'll have this first novel done in no time.

Especially with my newfound inspiration.

CHAPTER 7

rett

THE FIRST WEEK and a half on the job is mostly uneventful. I get into a nice little daily routine.

I arrive to work earlier than everyone else. Seven is early enough for this, since most of the office rolls in around seven thirty or eight. I check my emails for around ten or fifteen minutes and take care of anything pressing.

Around seven thirty or eight, I pull up my google doc and write my book for about an hour. As the rest of the office gradually arrives and takes their desks, I smile internally at all of the head nods I get.

Wow, that girl is here so early and working.

Yes, that's right. I'm working extra hard.

On my romance novel.

And my inspiration, well let's just say, it doesn't hurt to have a hot boss on the same floor.

Yes, I admit it--in spite of Sebastian's asshole-ish reputation, I have a building attraction for how he looks in a suit.

Sebastian's not there every day, since some days he's traveling. But on the days he is there, I feel a connection and, *on edge* isn't exactly the right term. It's actually a bit frustrating that I can't put the right word on how I feel about us.

Friday morning, I'm writing a particularly sexy scene at the beginning of my book. The female hero, who I've named Lacy, hasn't hooked up with her boss Zane yet. But the sexual tension is palpable for Zane and Lacy. It's a very over-the-top scene about when she drops a pen in his office and does a little bending-and-snapping to get it à la Legally Blonde, the movie with Reese Witherspoon. She turns and gauges his reaction--and catches a little glint of naughtiness in his eye. Zane doesn't have his tie on today like usual--just a suit coat. And he's got an extra button that he's taken down that leaves Lacy wondering if *maybe, just maybe* she's got a chance with the man everyone in her world wants.

But the question remains, why would Zane want little Lacy?

I take a sip of my coffee, then sigh deeply and toss my head back a little, resting my hands on the keyboard.

Why am I even writing this novel? Do I really think their romance is realistic? What is it with me and guys in positions of power?

In my mind's eye, my muse appears. If there ever was a muse in my life for a powerful, attractive man, it's so obvious who it would be: Sebastian Blackwell.

Sebastian Blackwell, the man who I had a crush on when I worked as a server at age fifteen and he was the owner of the restaurant.

The only billionaire Blackwell has ever had to my knowledge. He's got it all--young, rich, and handsome.

I consider the next words I'm writing in my book, and I

wonder, really: what makes a man like Sebastian settle down? Does he just look for the hottest woman available and date her, like the Instagram model Crystal showed me? Or is there something else he takes into consideration?

I glance at the clock on my computer. Eight-twenty. Not quite enough time to write another full scene before the others in the office arrive. Should Lacy and Zane hook up already?

No. I'm going to toy with them a little bit more. I'll just end this scene with some heavy sexual tension.

As I begin to type the scene, the air goes out of me when I hear the voice behind me.

"What are you working on, Brett?"

I whip my head around and see Sebastian standing holding his coffee, smirking ever so slightly.

"Excuse me?" I say, trying not to gasp.

"I said you're here early. You always are. It's impressive. You'd be surprised how few employees even come in one minute earlier than they have to. So I'm just curious what you're working on."

"I was...checking on some emails, and I sort of figured I'd write a report," I say, doing my best to contain my nervousness and shaky voice.

"Oh," he says, his voice still full of that deep morning timbre. "What sort of report?"

I feel my face tingle a little as I hesitate.

"It's a document detailing the themes that Blackwell farmers are most likely to open us to us about. Like, a cheat sheet," I lie.

"Oh. A cheat sheet. Well thank you for your extra effort."

"Anything for you."

"Is everything going well with Bob? He can be a handful, I know. But he means well."

I minimize the document I'm working on so my emails

show up, then spin out of my chair and stand up, grabbing a pen out of nervousness. "Bob's fine," I say. "I sometimes get confused by his directions, though."

"Really? Why's that?"

"Well." I shrug, fiddling with the pen. "Like the twenty-calls-every-morning rule. It makes no sense to me. We don't track the numbers to make sure they are in the system. I could literally call twenty of my friends--making sure they have the Blackwell county area code--and I'd have my calls done for the day. Obviously I don't do that. But I think when we're talking about dealing with these small town farmers, we don't want to be barraging them with phone calls. We're better off having quality conversations and getting to know them."

Sebastian doesn't say anything for a few seconds, as if checking to make sure I'm done speaking. He has a habit of being silent for a few beats after I--or most people--finish their sentences. This puts me on edge, so I keep talking.

"So, I get to work early just to make sure I'm in a relaxed mood and have my emails done, so I can worry about the calls. They stress me out a little, if I'm being honest."

Sebastian nods. "Cold calling can be tough. But you were hired for a reason. You're spectacular with people. I'm sure you get that all the time, though."

My cheeks flush red and I twirl the pen in my hand even harder.

"Thanks," is all I say. We share a moment in silence.

Sebastian's dark brown eyes flash around the sales floor. He takes another drink of coffee, and his neck flexes. I wonder if he's stressed out. How could a man run a multi-billion dollar enterprise and *not* be stressed out?

Yet he seems so calm and collected all the time.

It's an ungodly attractive combination. I take another sip of my coffee.

Sebastian stares into me with his mocha brown eyes.

And I stare back at him.

Shoot. I panic a little, silently. Am I being awkward? He knows I was looking at him before in his office. Can he know I have a little baby crush on him?

No. Just because he's a billionaire doesn't mean he can read minds. He's probably this nice to all of his employees.

My pen-twirling starts to break records, and I drop the thing on the carpet, right at Sebastian's feet.

Without thinking, I bend down to grab it, and before I have the time to realize what I'm doing, my face is damn near in Sebastian's crotch as I pick the thing up.

I don't think he sees it, but my jaw drops a little as I get up close and personal with his *thing.*

That's gotta be the pleats. No way is that his...cucumber.

And then I swear it moves. Something between his legs *moves*.

I snap my head back up, and for a brief second, our eyes meet.

"My pen fell," is all I can say, and I do my best not to let a look of absolute fright take over.

Sebastian smirks. "Brett, I don't even know what to do with you." He shakes his head and laughs, his laughter booming through the floor. A few other employees glance over.

"You can give me a raise since I'm awesome." I wink, trying to distract our conversation from the fact that I just clearly checked out my boss's crotch.

"I think you're the one who'll be giving me a raise." He winks, and as if realizing what he just insinuated, he quickly follows it up. "By closing some deals this week!"

"I should get back to work," he says. "But I'm serious about this, Brett. If you ever need anything--you just let me know. I realize the sales floor is eighty percent male, and sometimes the guys can be a bit much. I want you to be as comfortable as possible here, so you can do your thing. You've got a lot of talent. I can't teach talent. But I can maximize it. I'm serious--my door is always open. For anything you need."

"Anything?" I say, my heart beating faster than it should be.

"Anything." He glances over his shoulder and rakes a hand through his hair. "I gotta go. See you later, Killer."

I spin back into my chair, my heart beating a million miles a minute. Was I imagining it, or was that conversation laced with some serious flirtation?

I pull my novel back up with a sigh.

Lacy is so sexy and smooth when she bends and snaps. Why am I so dang awkward?

I guess real life is never as smooth as romance novels.

I glance around the office one more time, and the cubicles around me are still mostly empty. Probably because it's a Friday, people are taking their time arriving to work. Good. Because what I'm about to do, no one can see.

I run a hand up my thighs, under my skirt. I touch my panties, and my suspicion is confirmed.

I'm not just wet. I'm soaked through.

This is going to be an interesting work day.

CHAPTER 8

Sebastian

"YOUR SHIH TZU IS TAKING A SHIT," Liam says, glancing at me with a smug look.

"I'm sure that's a joke that's never ever been made before," I say, trying not to crack a smile.

"Yeah? So what? It's still hilarious."

Sundays, I usually do something with my family. This morning, I meet up with my brother Liam and we walk a couple of dogs from the local dog shelter around town. Today we stroll around the campus quad of Blackwell University.

"And your lab is...labbing? Fuck. It doesn't work the other way." I shake my head as I stare down the dog Liam snagged.

"That's right. My dog is fucking awesome. Yes you are Shiloh!" He pets the chocolate lab and the dog gets into it, wagging his tail out of control. "Just admit I'm the king of dirty dog puns. Bow at how good of a master I am."

"You know, it's good I have a brother like you," I say as I tie off the doggie bag and toss it in a nearby trash can. "If not, I'd probably get a big head."

"You do have a big head." Liam winks. "I mean literally."

I nod as we stroll down the quad. "You got me there. A big head for big brains. Thank God I have the money for these custom fitted hats," I say, switching my baseball cap around to wear it backwards.

"I have some news," Liam says. "I need to tell someone. I figure since you're my brother, you're forced to listen."

"Seriously?"

He nods, almost gravely. My brother's not one to get serious--he almost never says a straight line. So I listen while he tells me about how he's falling for a girl.

Well, *fell* is a better word. But their relationship, if you could call it that, leaves me flabbergasted.

"Let me get this straight," I say, holding up a hand. Both dogs turn and look at me, as if they realize I'm about to make a very important proclamation. "You had a one-night stand. With a client."

He shrugs. "When you put it like that, it seems wrong. I was helping her out. She was in a tough spot."

"So you...gave her a hand?" I wink. "Did you get her engine up and running?"

"Hey," Liam barks back. "This is my love you are talking about here. Be careful. And of course I did. She was up and purring in no time. The engine, I mean. The engine was purring."

I toss my head back in laughter. My brother is an asshole and a lady killer. I'm honestly a little surprised to hear him talking about a girl like he's talking about Haley. But I guess even the Liam's of the world have to settle down sometime.

"What about you, big bro?" he asks. "You gonna settle down sometime soon?"

The question catches me a little off guard. I run my hand along my jawline and we start walking again.

"Me?" I scoff. "I don't have time for a woman. You know that. It would end badly."

"What, because you're 'building your empire?'"

"Yes," I nod.

Liam shrugs as we turn down another part of the University quad. "Man, I got news for you: that empire you always dreamed about: it's built now. Look around, man! Who donated the money for the new Art Center for Blackwell U?"

I shrug. "I did."

"Right. Man, whose nonprofit did we pick up these dogs at? You own this town. What else do you want?"

"Maybe I'm just not the kind of guy who's meant to have a long-term relationship," I say. "Flings are more my thing. Man, what the hell, just at the beginning of the summer you were talking about how great being single was, and how you'd never settle down. What changed?"

Liam swallows, looks me in the eye. "Haley."

I nod, and I understand what he means by that. "Well, I guess I just haven't found my Haley yet," I say.

Liam shrugs. "Hey man, maybe you're not. Maybe you'll never find her. I get it, I've been there. But I can tell you from personal experience--that shit happens when you are least looking for it. You don't even have any candidates?"

I chuckle. "No, I don't have any--"

I stop myself, because the word candidates makes me think of résumé. And résumé makes me think of my recent hires.

And that leads me to the girl who I've been doing my damnedest not to flirt with at work.

Brett Blue.

"Awww shit," Liam drawls. "I know that face! Big brother's got a crush. Yes he does, doesn't he, Shiloh?" He bends down and pets the dog furiously, and Shiloh leans in, clearly loving it. "Goddamn this dog is awesome! I just might have to bring him home with me. So who's the lucky girl?"

"There is no girl." I try to say the words in a serious voice, but they come out weird.

"Ha! Dude, you act like I haven't known you since you were born."

"I was born before you," I smirk.

"Okay, twenty-eight years. You're twenty-nine now, right?"

I chuckle. "Come on, you don't know your own brother's age."

Liam looks a little flustered. He continues. "The point is I know when to call bullshit on my own brother. And I call bullshit. You sound like Keanu Reeves in the Matrix." Liam whips off his sunglasses, feigns holding a utensil in front of his eyes, and says in his best Keanu Reeves voice. "There is no spoon."

"Fuck you, man. Fine. You want to know? We have this new girl...and I can't get her off my mind. She's a whip-smart new hire from outside the city limits. Something about her, man. She drives me nuts. Every interaction we have, I'm like 'is she flirting with me? Or is this just coincidence.'"

"Please, bro. Give me the down low."

"Her name is Brett Blue." I start to say something else, but Liam holds up a hand.

"Wait a second. *Her* name is Brett? That's not even close to a girl's name."

"It's her dad's middle name, and she used to be quite a tomboy. Anyways, yesterday I stopped by her desk and she was acting weird. I couldn't put my finger on how, exactly. Then she dropped a pen right at my feet, and when she picked it up, she stole a cock glance."

Liam's jaw drops. "She stole a look at the Blackwell family jewels?"

"That's right."

"You're sure of it."

"I think so, man. Fuck, who knows. Maybe I imagined it."

"If she did--bro--she likes you. No doubt about it. Damn, I'm gonna have to look this girl up. New hire eh? So...why don't you just ask her out?"

I smile, because I envy Liam's simple solution-making. "Dude, it's not that simple. I run a billion-dollar company. I can't just go around asking my employees out. I have a reputation to uphold. That might be okay in the auto shop, but we have an HR department. I don't want to make her uncomfortable, you know?"

Liam runs a hand through his hair. "I see your point. Shit man, I don't know. Just look for the signals. She'll probably leave you an opening if she wants you."

"That's what she said." I wink, and Liam tosses his head back in laughter.

"Ahh, you motherfucker. See, what do you need my help for? You got this covered. Ain't that right, Shiloh?"

The dog turns and looks back at us, and I swear he winks at me.

I can't tell if that's a good or a bad omen.

CHAPTER 9

rett

Monday morning, I make a new discovery about having a 'real' office job:

Unscheduled Monday morning meetings are the worst.

I sit and nod as my manager Bob flips through the power point, briefing the team on slides of the different areas around Blackwell that we are focusing our strategy on buying up. Having lived here all my life, I could be up there presenting and probably doing a better job than Bob.

Instead, I'm sitting at the last possible seat of the long, boardroom table, and not listening to one word of Bob's monotone voice.

I squint toward the front of the room and nod, feigning attention, while I write down notes on my note pad.

Except none of my notes have anything to do with the PowerPoint. Instead, I'm wondering how Lacy is going to hook up with her boss Zane now that they've broken the ice.

I glance around the boardroom. There are plenty of fun places to do it in here.

Lacy's fingers pressed against the glass as he does her from behind. Ohh yeah.

Bent over on the desk. Also from behind.

Hmm. I need some variation. Zane's a jacked boss, so he'll have no problem scooping her up and setting her on the desk and doing her normal-style. Yes, not quite missionary, because she's sitting and he's standing.

Is that what that's called? Just 'normal-style?' Seems like there ought to be a better word for it.

Better word for 'normal-style' I jot down on my notepad.

What else could they do? Well with how dominant Zane is, I imagine he'd want to have his way with Lacy and own every inch of her. He'd probably want to finger fuck her on her back while her head hangs off the table.

But is Lacy ready for that? She's definitely a dirty girl, but only with the right man.

Zane needs to earn that, I decide, and jot down another note.

Dirtier later

How realistic is it that they would really hook up in a place like this big boardroom and not get caught? The frosted glass starts about two feet above the floor. Lacy and Zane definitely can't do any fucking on the floor unless the office is totally empty.

I bite my lower lip. Wow, the ideas are really flowing today. Why is that?

I swallow, because I certainly know why.

Sebastian Blackwell. I can't get him off my mind. How would he be with a girl like Lacy? Lacy is just his type, the way I've described her in the book so far. She's secretly an Instagram model, with a perfect hourglass figure, like the girl that Crystal showed me. Sebastian would take her straight away, he wouldn't wait to be dirty with her. During their first encounter, I bet he'd rip her panties right off, bend her over, and take her like it was his last.

A wave of heat comes over me as I let my imagination run wild for just a second. Sebastian bending her over, fucking her, slapping her ass cheeks with his hand while he thrusts into her, slapping her with his strong hips.

Except in the fantasy, Lacy disappears for a moment.

I appear.

I don't want anyone else being with Sebastian.

I want him all to myself.

"Miss Blue. Miss Blue?" a voice says, sounding far away.

Holy shit. I space in and realize Bob's calling my name.

"Yes?"

"Wondering what you thought about the question I just asked you," Bob says condescendingly, crossing his arms.

My face warms and turns bright red. I have no clue what Bob is asking me, and the entire room is staring at me.

"Well, I uh." I clear my throat.

A deep voice cuts me off from behind me.

"Ladies and gentlemen, it's almost ten a.m. I think we had better wrap it up."

Sebastian glances at his watch and then back at the rest of us.

Was he standing behind me the entire time?

Bob seems annoyed, like he was hoping to call me out in front of everyone.

"Let's hit the floor people!" Sebastian says with a smile. "I want to hear some dials. Let's drum up some business today. We have a lot of work to do this week."

Sebastian claps his hands a few times and starts talking to another employee in the vicinity. Bob huffs toward me, clearly unhappy. Before I can close my notepad, he zooms in and slaps his palms down on one of the pages.

"Let's see what kind of notes you were taking. Maybe I can help you."

My heart about jumps up to my throat. I feel like I'm a girl about to be thrown in detention, not someone with a mature full-time job.

"No, didn't really take any," I say, and attempt to close my notebook. Instead, Bob takes it from me and looks at it up close.

I'd giggle if I weren't so worried what Bob will say about my notes, which I'm sure make no sense to him. As I suspect, he rubs a forefinger and thumb on his forehead as he tries to make sense of what I wrote.

"'Better word for normal-style?'" he reads out loud, and his eyes dart to mine. His face is full of confusion. "What on Earth does that mean?"

I shrug. "Just something I was thinking about."

"'Dirtier...later?' Okay now that one you're gonna have to explain to me."

I stand up, nervously looking up to Bob. He's heavyset, and not really intimidating, but the fact that he's got the power exasperates me. "I was just writing, if I ever have a meeting with one of the farmers later in the day, they are going to be covered in more dirt. So we should take that into account if we're heading out to a farm site."

Bob scratches the side of his thinning head of hair. "*That's* what you were thinking about during this meeting?"

Sebastian, as if by sixth sense, notices the tension in the air, and calmly wheels around after ending his conversation with the other employee.

"Bob. Brett. Everything alright here?"

"No, everything's *not* alright," Bob emphasizes. "Look at these notes she's taking." He hands him my notebook, and again, I feel like my work is being passed from teacher to principal.

"Hmm. Interesting. Bob, why don't you head outside? I'll take care of this."

Bob shoots me a smug look like he won, and heads outside, leaving Sebastian and I alone in the big boardroom.

My gaze shoots to his big hands as he hands the notebook back to me. "Truthfully, I don't give a fuck what you write in here if you're closing deals," he says, and shakes his head a little bit. "I'll be honest, I *am* curious what those notes mean. But I'm not worried about it. All of the greatest CEOs and geniuses wrote weird notes to themselves."

"Are you telling me I'm a genius?"

"You're quite smart, Brett. That much is evident to anyone with half a brain. You've got the brains, and the beauty."

I swallow. "Thank you."

"It's a deadly combination in sales. I expect a lot out of you. And hey, you let me know about Bob. If he's getting too out of it. He's going through a divorce--tough time for him."

"Oh. I didn't know that."

"Keep it on the downlow. Alright, anyways, I'll see you later...dirtier." He winks.

"Excuse me?"

He chuckles. "Your note. Dirtier later."

"Ohh!" I cackle, apparently having the memory of a dog. It's not my fault that I practically wilt in front of this man.

Sebastian swallows, and I wonder what it would be like to be dirtier--*now*--with him.

We head to the front of the room, and there just happens to be a basket full of Now and Laters on the edge of the table. "What's your favorite flavor?" Sebastian asks, pulling out a couple.

"Cherry," I say.

"Here you go," he says, tossing one at me.

He turns off the lights as we head out the door, and I pop the cherry taffy into my mouth.

* * *

THE NEXT DAY, I close my first deal, buying a property to the east of Blackwell. Convincing the man wasn't hard once he knew I was a local and I wasn't trying to gyp him, just offer him a fair price to help him retire. I turn the deal over to our legal team, and there's suddenly an air of awe from the people around me. Even Bob is impressed.

"No one has ever closed a property deal in their first month," Bob comes over and tells me, his eyes wide with wonder.

I shrug. "They have now."

I beam with some pride, but the truth is, I wouldn't have been able to sell those properties if I weren't Brett Blue's daughter. Every call I make, when they ask me who I am, I don't say "Brett from Blackwell Industries," I just say "Brett Blue," and they open up to me in ways they'd never open up to some of my colleagues, a few of whom are transplants from nearby big cities.

Since I've got my big sale out of the way, I decide to give myself the gift of writing more of my book. Knowing my boss will be off my back for once helps me to concentrate on what I really want to do: writing my romance novel.

I find it amazing that in a big company like Blackwell Industries, I can work at this for one or two hours a day and no one blinks an eye. On the other hand, my coworker Ed goes on fantasy football websites for probably the same amount of time during the day. So what difference does it make if I write?

I stay later, past seven, writing all the while. All of a sudden, it's eight p.m., the air conditioning in the building shuts off, and I realize I'm totally, completely alone in the building. I look at the calendar--September seventeenth.

My father passed away on the seventeenth of June--three months ago to the date. I wonder what he'd make of all this, me working at a company like Blackwell Industries. His dream was always for one of us to take over his farm, but I just don't know if it's in the cards.

I finish writing a scene where Lacy and her boss Zane finally kiss. She leans into him after a meeting, and he grabs her up against the wall and makes out with her.

Damn. I could use a make out session right about now. And plus, I'm extra worked up from writing this scene.

I decide that rather than go directly home, I want to make use of this pent-up energy and work out using the building gym.

When I arrive to the fifth-floor workout room, the lights are off and the gym is completely empty. No one is on the treadmills, on the weights, or even in the hardwood room for abs and biking. I change into my yoga pants and a tank top, run a few minutes to warm up, then do a few arm exercises. There's a wall mirror, and I check myself out in it.

I want to get a bigger ass--one of those 'Instagram asses' like the girl Sebastian was with in the picture Crystal showed me.

I giggle. 'Instagram ass.' I'll definitely put that term in the book.

I pull up YouTube and look at some butt workout videos. Apparently, squats and deadlifts are the thing to do. I chide myself for not remembering that from my high school soccer practices.

I decide to have some fun with it. I throw some music on my phone, blasting Fifth Harmony as loud as I can through my speaker. I put just a little bit of weight on the bar, and do some squats.

After a couple of sets, I change up the music and throw on a little "Blurred Lines."

I watch the music video for a minute on my phone, and I can't help it. I start dancing a little bit around the gym like the actress in the music video. Then I do some squats and some deadlifts to the beat, being extremely silly, and not even really knowing why.

I smile to myself, thinking how this is kind of me and Sebastian's song. How blurred are our lines?

I wouldn't mind blurring them a little more. Sebastian is too classy for that, though. I'm pretty darn sure.

As the song is coming to an end, I freeze, thinking I hear something or someone else in the gym. I spin around, but don't see a thing.

My endorphins must be humming, or maybe it's the dancing I was doing. I head back into the ladies' locker room to take a shower, since I'm super sweaty. My good vibes are interrupted when I turn the shower on and it fizzles out quickly.

I sigh, and come up with a plan. No one is here. The lights are even dimmed in the weight room. The chances of another person being here are slim to none, so why can't I just use the men's shower?

Wrapped in a towel, I grab my gym bag and sneak outside into the weight room, then head into the men's locker room.

As I enter, I see a pair of shoes neatly sitting before one locker. Maybe someone left them overnight?

Still, I proceed into the locker room because I don't hear a thing. But when I turn the corner, I drop my jaw at what I see in the shower stall.

Sebastian Blackwell stands in it, without the water on, pumping his big hard cock with one fist, eyes closed as he leans with the other hand against the wall. I'd seen him before, but this is something else.

I can't help staring at him, my eyes wide. His wide shoulders narrow to a V, the veins of his abs and six pack so yummy I want to reach right over this blurred line and lick him.

I swallow, watching him for just this one instant. He jerks his head up, and I'm afraid he might see me, so I duck around the corner, hiding on the other side of the cinder block walls.

Now all I can hear is his grunting, his hard breathing, and the slick sound of skin on skin as he has it out with himself in the shower.

I wonder what he's thinking about?

I hop up on the sink. From my position, if he walks out from the shower, I'll hear him and have at least five seconds to slip out of the bathroom before he can lurch around the corner and see me. I glance down at my gym bag, my black Blackwell University cap sticking out of the top of the bag.

I'm so turned on from his sounds. I can't help it. I ask myself the most ridiculous question ever. And I am a girl who has a history of asking herself ridiculous questions.

What would Lacy do?

My legs swinging as I sit on the sink countertop, I put two fingers on my clit and lean back, rubbing myself. I'm already so wet and turned on.

Lacy would walk right over to him and ask him something sexy, like 'can I give you a hand with that?'

Zane would smile, a little surprised, but he's a man who knew this was inevitable given the sparks that I have been creating between the two of them.

He'd frame her ass just right against the wall. He'd start the encounter by kneeling and diving between her legs with his tongue, getting her warmed up.

Oh sweet Lord. I rub my fingers over my slickness and resist moaning. I refocus on Sebastian. I can still hear him grunting and growling a little. And that slick, wet sound of him taking his cock in his hand. I wonder if he's sliding his own precum on his cock? I wonder how it would taste?

Then Zane would put his hand on her back, sliding his thick cock into her wet pussy from behind, slowly entering her inch by inch.

I slide my fingers into my tight heat. I bite my lip as I picture Zane fucking Lacy.

No, screw that. I know what I'm thinking about. I let my imagination run with what I really want. *Sebastian lays into me with his thick cock. I feel his muscular abs, his strong hips pound into me again and again.*

I stifle a moan. My hips gyrate as I come.

Holy shit. I listen for a moment, and all I hear is the sound of my own breath.

The shower turns on for a minute, then it stops. I put two and two together.

Sebastian just came, and now he's showering.

The shower stops.

Oh fuck. I need to get out of here.

I scramble to grab my gym bag, and run out of the gym room in a flurry. I throw my yoga pants, shirt, and shoes back on as quickly as I can in the ladies' locker room, and I decide I'll shower at home.

The elevator dings, and I make it to my car.

Talk about blurred lines.

I make it out of there without a trace. Thank God.

CHAPTER 10

Sebastian

On Wednesday morning, I stroll into work with a whistle and some pep in my step. I crank out my morning pull ups, pushups, and sit-ups. The sun rises on the horizon just like any normal day.

Well, about as normal as any day could be after you caught your hottest female employee watching you jerk off in the men's bathroom of the gym.

Okay, let's take it back a step. I wouldn't say she 'caught' me like I was doing something I was ashamed of. Besides, it's her fault I was masturbating in the shower. It's not something I do--ever--at work.

But when I peeked into the hardwood room for a moment, I saw Brett doing squats and deadlifts in those black pants that were sculpted perfectly to her ass. As she performed the movements of the squat she awakened a part of me dormant for too long--the risky, sexual part of me.

And instead of getting my late Tuesday workout in like I had planned, I was unusually worked up. So I had myself a shower session.

Can you blame me? I mean, have you ever seen a guy try to work out with a giant boner that won't go away? It's damn near impossible. So I figured I'd work myself out before working out.

If the bathrooms had surveillance cameras, I would have commandeered those and figured out what she was doing in the men's bathroom. While I was cranking my cock in the shower, I thought I heard the faintest of moans. I figured it was just my own imagination doing its thing as I pictured fucking Brett against the shower wall.

Okay, you got me. I pictured her. An employee. Is that against work policy to picture someone? Of course not. We can't judge people on what's in their heads.

Hey, if she didn't leave her Blackwell University cap--and if I didn't instantly recognize her smell in the cap she left behind--I might have never suspected it was her.

I take a sip of my morning joe, open up my email inbox, and get to work. I stare at the screen, but I feel like I'm looking at Chinese. I can't concentrate worth a shit.

I scrub a hand across my newly clean-shaven face and a burst of mischievousness fills me. Brett comes in every day, earlier than almost every employee. And now she stays late? She must be working double what one of my normal employees do.

Curious, I pull up the phone statistics to check. Every employee is expected to make thirty-five calls and talk on the phone for two hours.

Brett's statistics are one hour on the phone and twenty-five calls per day, below average.

So what the hell is she doing with her time? Online shopping? Why is she here so late?

Something doesn't add up with her. What about those veiled notes she took during our meeting yesterday. 'Better word for normal-style?' and 'dirtier later?'

As I run my forefinger and thumb on my forehead, I remember we are running a new employee work efficiency software. It's a little creepy how much data we can get from our employees. It even records the number of clicks and keystrokes they make per day, as well as the time their desktop is powered on. Personally, I don't like encroaching on people's privacy, but I also need to know where the weak points in the company are.

I pull up the rest of Brett's statistics. Her keystroke number is way out of whack. I stare in disbelief at the amount, and I have to wonder if the software is somehow wrong.

Her keystrokes are *quadruple* her nearest competitor.

What the fuck? Is she writing a damn novel?

I check my watch. Seven thirty, and at this time, Brett's almost always sitting at her desk typing away. I decide to cross a little bit of a line. I go to the surveillance mainframe and pull up her desktop computer, so I see in real time what she's doing. My screen becomes her screen.

She's got a google document pulled up. And she's typing something. A very long document. Curious, I scroll up and read her words.

"LACY," Zane breaths. "What the fuck are you doing here?"

Zane pants like he's out of breath. His huge cock still in his hand, we make eye contact.

I swallow, nervousness expanding through my chest. I've never been a ballsy girl. But what I'm about to say might change that.

"Zane," I mutter, dropping my towel in front of him. His eyes drift to my tits, then back up to my face. I take a few steps toward

him until I'm basically standing in the shower, close to him. I can feel the heat emanating from his body. I reach out and put a delicate hand on those delicious abs I've been waiting to rub. "Can I...give you a hand?"

He cocks his chin up, and runs his eyes over my whole body, as if savoring my response.

"Yes. Fuck yes."

He rubs his hand on my wrist, gently bringing me toward him. Electricity shoots down my spine as we cross the imaginary line between boss and employee. He's so tall, my tits rub against his abs as we embrace. He turns the faucet of the shower, and the warm water runs over our bodies as we kiss for one, two, three minutes. I lose track of time. While he nibbles on my lower lip, I run my hand down his wet side, searching for his cock. It's so prominent, his erection sticking straight out. It's not hard to find. He groans as I grip him, gently at first.

Zane pulls back from my neck for a moment, and fists my hair in his hand, forcing me to look him in the eye. "I've wanted you so badly since you walked through that door," Zane growls. "You have no idea."

"Me too," I whisper back.

His moans intensify as I stroke back and forth tighter on his cock, using his precum juices to slide across my clit with ease.

"Turn around," Zane mouths. "I'm going to fuck you so good, you have no idea."

Dear fucking God.

I blink a few times in utter disbelief, then give my cheek a few pats for good measure.

Is Brett writing an erotic novel in her downtime at work?

And is it just me, or is she basically writing about what *would* have happened if she and I hooked up?

This is too much for a Wednesday morning.

"Speaking of hump day," I mutter, glancing down at the tent I've pitched in my charcoal grey suit, compliments of Brett's fucking writing.

Pun intended.

Brett seemed so innocent when I hired her. Tiny. Blonde. From the heart of the heartland. Where the hell is she getting the inspiration and deciding that she wants to be an erotic author?

I rake a hand through my hair, and I decide this calls for some swift, decisive action.

I rise up from my desk and first do a few pushups to get rid of the Ron Burgundy style erection I've got going on, minus the pleats.

Move along folks. Nothing to see here.

When I'm finally satisfied my bulge has gone down, I grab my coffee and head out onto the sales floor.

The CEO doesn't need to make an appearance every day, but it's always good to know he's there. Keeps the morale of the troops high.

Except today, I have a very specific target for my morning walk.

It's five to eight now, and about half of the desks are filled up. I walk over to Bob's desk. He's not there yet, no big surprise. I've been meaning to have a little chat with him about general productivity.

I stroll casually down one aisle, careful to walk out of Brett's eyesight.

Finally, I turn and see her cubicle, watching her from about twenty feet away. I see her, but she can't see me. I stride silently toward her. I become a Jedi knight. Luckily the three desks in her pod are unoccupied. Perfecto.

I take a moment to smile her way, admiring her spirit. The truth is, writing erotica on the clock is drastically against company policy. She should immediately be fired.

But, honestly, I highly respect anyone who believes that much in an idea of theirs to work hard at it. The vast majority of my employees just play with their iPhones, check their Twitter, go on Facebook, and look at Fantasy football statistics for a minimum of one to two hours per day. Those are just the facts.

Brett's got a vision for her free time, at least.

A very hot vision.

Her blonde hair falls just beyond her shoulders. Today she's got on this white and red strappy dress, emphasizing her cute arms.

Did I just say cute arms?

Well it's true. She's a beautiful creature, from her shoulders, to her arms, to her neck...and of course that magnificent ass that spurred me to choke my chicken in the shower yesterday. As I approach, I can sense her fresh scent. It's like blueberries and bluebonnets mixed together. Even the way she *sits* is gorgeous. All prim and proper and southern belle-like. I wonder what she'd do if I just upped and kissed her on the neck, right now, with no warning.

I marvel at her typing speed. She's in the zone, furiously writing her shower sex scene.

As soon as I arrive behind her, I clear my throat. "Morning, Miss Blue."

I've never seen someone minimize a screen so fast in my life since my brother got caught by my mom watching porn when we were kids.

"Morning, Mr. Blackwell," she chokes, clicking onto her outlook email like she *wasn't just writing fucking erotica.*

I smile and take a breath. She half-spins her chair around, and I swear she glances ever so quickly at the bulge in my pants before she looks up at me.

"You're here early," I say, my voice coming out lower than usual. "That's good."

As she opens her mouth to speak, it's like our interaction is happening in slow motion.

"I always get here early." She smiles, and I notice a quiver of nerves in her voice.

"I'm glad you're here early. I wanted to talk with you about something important. Do you have a moment?"

As she goes to open her mouth, I go right past first base and head toward second. I wonder what it would feel like to have those soft sultry lips wrapped around my cock. Glancing out the window, I try to focus on anything but the sexy blonde in front of me.

"Yes, of course," she says without hesitation.

Damn, she's good. If I were just walked up on by my boss when I was writing erotica, I don't think I would be this calm and collected. Then again, I haven't been an employee for years, so I have no clue what it's like to have someone looking over your shoulder.

"I wanted to talk about your first couple of weeks. And how you're...spending your time here," I elaborate.

That gets a reaction out of her. It's barely perceptible, but I see the mini-muscles in her face contract, giving me evidence of her nervousness under that confident veneer.

"Great, what's up?"

I swallow, and smile. I was going to just come right out and tell her I know about the little side project she's been working on. But what fun is that? I call an audible.

"Bob's sometimes a little overbearing," I say instead. "I noticed your interaction at the meeting yesterday. Is everything okay?"

She swallows. "With Bob? Oh, yes. I mean, not completely. He's a good man, but sometimes I feel like he's picking on me."

I rock back on my heel and take a sip of my coffee. "I'll be honest. Bob didn't used to be quite like this when I hired him. I think his home situation is leaking into his work. That being said, he doesn't have an excuse to call you out like he did in the meeting yesterday."

"You noticed that too? So I'm not crazy."

"No. You're not crazy at all. That's why I stepped in. Although, I am curious to what your little notes meant."

She shrugs. "I sometimes write weird notes. Just a weird thing I do."

"Okay." I glance at my watch. "Shoot, I have to go, I have an eight o'clock."

"Okay. Thanks," she says, and her voice is laced with some of that moan I swear I heard yesterday in the bathroom.

I turn halfway around, and I notice her looking up at the ceiling and the heavens, like she just dodged a bullet.

"Oh and Brett," I say, looking over my shoulder.

"Yeah?"

I pause for a few beats, letting the air become awkward. Does she know that I know what she's doing with her free time?

Fuck it. I want to keep this a secret for just a little longer. I'll keep this ace in the hole, and use it at just the right time.

"Great job closing your first deal yesterday. Very impressive."

With that, I walk off back into my office.

"Fiona, cancel my eight o'clock," I say.

"Oh? Did something come up?"

"Yes," I smirk. "Something very important."

I enter my office, shut the door, and open a word doc.

I start writing.

So Brett wants to play a little cat-and-mouse?

I'll play this game all day long.

CHAPTER 11

rett

ON THURSDAY MORNING, I get to work and I write like always. I'm quite happy with the little system I've devised. Write, work, write, work, throughout the day. Lacy and Zane provide me with a nice little distraction from my own work.

At a quarter to eight, I head down the elevator and outside to grab some coffee. When I sit down back at my desk, I notice something is off. There is a little piece of paper sticking out of the bottom of my keyboard, which seems shifted.

I put my coffee down, snatch the piece of paper, and read. It's a hand-scribbled note:

Zane and Lacy should hook up in one of the janitor closets. Those things are big.

P.S. - Lacy seems hot, why isn't she blonde, though?

P.P.S. - You should check your document. I added a section to it.

My heart hammers through my blouse. Who knows? Who is playing a trick on me?

Suddenly, everyone's a suspect. I stand up, and glance at the guy a few rows down from me, who appears to have just arrived. Bob walks in, looking disheveled as always.

I take a deep breath, and sit back down at my desk. Once Bob is seated, and I'm satisfied he won't be randomly stopping by my desk, I sit down and open my desktop back up and pull up my email.

There's an email that just says 'from x@blackwellindustries.com.'

I curiously open the email and read, slack-jawed.

"So this is what we're reduced to?" Lacy says with a smile, her baby blues a warming the cockles of my heart. "The janitor's closet?"

"Reduced to?" I smirk. "Don't act like you've never wanted to hook up in one of these. This is hot. Look at all the tools we have around here." I pick up a mop and hold it, smiling. "We could really have some fun with this."

Lacy rolls her eyes as she unbuttons my shirt. She smiles.

"I think there's another big, long item in here I'd rather have fun with," she says.

She rolls her hand down my abdomen, my white shirt finally undone. She slips her hand further down and grabs hold of my rapidly hardening erection.

I groan, take the back of her head, and pull her into me for a deep kiss while she works to undo my belt buckle.

"Fuck, Lacy, those lips taste so good," I growl. "But not as good as this pussy's gonna taste." My fingers drift down her ass, and I

cup her butt over the cloth of her sexy white pants. My other hand drifts up her shirt, sliding under her bra. The makeout is sloppy, it's sweaty. And it's oh-so-fucking-hot, feeling Lacy's heat against me.

We look each other in the eye, and I can tell she's feral and on the brink of losing control. Just like me.

I unbutton her white pants and slide them off. They stick on her heels, and she goes to unbuckle them.

"Leave the heels on," I command.

Once her creamy thighs are revealed to me, I can't take anymore. I hoist her up onto the convenient waist-high stool and slide her panties off. I dive between her legs, flicking my tongue over her clit, and it tastes every bit as heavenly as I imagined. She comes at least once, quivering as I eagerly lap her up.

After a while, she grabs awkwardly at my cock until she finally grips it. "Please Zane. I want my boss to fuck me now. Make me purr."

How'd I do?

-Mr. X

P.S. - Pants changed to reflect the hottest girl in the office's pants color today. I was inspired.

MY EYES WIDEN at the screen. I'm frazzled, and, holy heck, I'm aroused by whoever wrote this. My heartbeat quickens and I can feel my pulse in my throat.

I look down at my pants, just to confirm I wasn't dreaming this morning when I put them on.

Yep. Still white.

I click off the email, and just in time, because Bob approaches my desk. I click onto another email, appearing very into whatever I'm reading.

"Morning, Brett!" Bob says, and he's got a little more of a skip in his step today.

"Hi Bob. Top o' the mornin' to you."

"We have an all-staff meeting at eight-thirty. Quarterly thing and all that jazz. Just wanted to make sure you have it on your calendar."

I pull up my email calendar. "I do. I have it right here. Thanks."

"Perfect." He turns to leave, but then spins back. "I almost forgot. There's something I need to tell you."

I swallow. Bob's look is mischievous. He has to be Mr. X.

"We're starting a task force," he says, taking his time with his words. "It's a cross-department team that will focus all of its efforts on completing the Blackwell Ranch project, and might bleed into the Shallowater distillery as well. It will have a few people from all teams. Sales, designers, suppliers, etc. Congratulations. Somebody high up likes you. Must be that sale you snagged this week."

"Sounds great," I say.

"Yep. You'll meet up on floor nine."

"Thanks. Well, I had better check a few more emails before that eight-thirty meeting."

THE ALL STAFF meeting is pretty boring, per usual. Mr. Blackwell's staff lawyer, Kim, is running it. It's mostly about mandatory company policy. Basically, they are talking to us to make sure Blackwell Industries is covered in the case of any type of lawsuit. I do notice that Kim shoots me a couple of weird looks throughout the meeting, but I don't think too much of them.

Once the meeting wraps up after about twenty-five minutes, I have just enough time to head to the meeting on floor nine.

I grab a seat at a round table, and seven other employees fill in the chairs around me. We introduce ourselves. Other than me and Kim, there's one other girl--the designer.

"Mr. Blackwell will be with us shortly," Kim says. "He's wrapping something up. But he wants me to thank all of you for being here and being a part of this task force."

A few minutes later, Sebastian enters. Today he wears a navy blue suit with a vest.

He hangs up his suit coat, and rolls up his sleeves.

"Alright y'all. It's time to hammer out some project details, and really get deep into this one. Blackwell Ranch is an ambitious undertaking, and we need all of us on the same page if we're going to get through this efficiently. You've all been chosen for one thing--talent and dedication."

He leans forward just a bit, setting his palms on the desk. I can't help but stare into Sebastian's dark brown eyes, the gorgeous things hidden under long eyelashes as he continues speaking.

"The work we're going to put in will be substantial. But as a reward, I'm providing each of you with a substantial stock-benefits package."

Troy, one of the younger sales guys seated around the table, raises his hand.

"Yes, Troy," Sebastian says, nodding at him.

"So there will be stock benefits. But Mr. Blackwell, will there be like any other *benefits?*" He winks.

Our little group cracks up, myself included.

Sebastian is smooth, and doesn't miss a beat with his response. "There are, of course, the added benefits of working on a team with a diverse group of individuals from different parts of the company. Throw in the fact that you'll get to work one on one with yours truly, and I'd say you have a whole slew of benefits, Troy. Any other questions?"

I swallow as Sebastian scans the faces of everyone in our group. When his eyes make contact with mine, electricity spikes through me as if the man can send a spark across the air between us. Seeing one on one before was hot, sure, but knowing how Sebastian can take control of a room is supreme sexy boss material.

I make a mental note that Zane is going to do it with Lacy after one such meeting.

"No more questions. Alright then. Schedules will be sent out. I look forward to seeing more of you all."

On the way out, Troy stops me. "Hey there," he says. "Troy."

"Brett," I say. "Nice to meet you."

Troy is the self-proclaimed 'bro' of the office. He's got an effortless charm about him, and two cute dimples. He pulls out a card and flashes an easy, natural smile.

"Here's my card. I know you're new around the office. Call me if you need anything. I'm happy to help you in any way I can."

"Oh. Well thanks. I don't have a card," I say as we reach the shiny silver elevator doors.

"That's the first thing I'd be happy to help you with," he says as we step in. "Email me and I'll tell you how to get your business cards made up for free."

"Okay," I say, and I have to smile because I think I just made my first office friend.

As the elevator doors close, I catch a glimpse of Sebastian's face, watching me curiously. I can't help flashing a smile back at him, wondering if he's jealous.

CHAPTER 12

rett

LATER THAT NIGHT, I'm waiting to go home, but the rain is pounding so hard outside I can't even see the buildings across the street, let alone think about driving.

I glance at my email, and a message is waiting for me in our Blackwell official messenger.

It's Mr. X.

Mr. X: It's really coming down outside.
Brett: Who are you?
Mr. X: Just a guy who's good with technology. And who loves to read your writing.
Brett: You're good with words, too. Did you really write that today?
Mr. X: What, a random guy can't have some writing skills?

Brett: Something tells me you're not a 'random' guy. What was your inspiration?
Mr. X: When I saw you today I couldn't help myself

My heart thumps hard, hammering through my blouse. I don't know if I should be upset or turned on.

The reality is I'm both. And I'm curious. I need to know who the heck this guy is.

Brett: It's raining
Mr. X: Yeah, really hard
Brett: Name the movie
Mr. X: Oh please. Mean Girls. You better believe I grew up on Lindsay Lohan.
Brett: I'm all done with my work for the day. I don't know what I'm going to do while I wait
Mr. X: I can think of a few special tasks for you to do
Brett: Yeah like what?
Mr. X: Well for starters you can eat the skittles I put next to your desk.

My eyes widen and I notice the bag of rainbow candies now next to me. I take the bag, open it, and put one in my mouth.

Mr. X: Huh. You're a strawberry girl. I wouldn't have guessed that
Brett: Holy shit. You're watching me
Mr. X: I'm not. Good idea though

I cross my legs. Then uncross them. My mouth dries and

my chest tightens. The sweet strawberry flavor of my red skittle spreads through my mouth.

Brett: I want to know who you are
  Mr. X: What and end our fun little game?
  Brett: There are other fun games we can play
  Mr. X: This one is so much fun though

I STAND UP, popping my head over the level of the cubicles so I can see if there are any other employees here. Only the secondary lights are on, and I see no one aside from the janitor.

I decide to take a gamble. I have a hunch who Mr. X is and I need to verify if my guess is right. I have flats on today, not heels, so I'm in stealth mode as I walk briskly on the carpet to Sebastian's office.

Fiona is gone, and as I approach I can see one light glowing in his office.

The door is open a crack, and I push it all the way open and proudly raise my voice as I enter.

"Gotcha!"

Terror spreads through me as I realize the room is totally empty. Thunder crashes outside, and I spin around in a panic to leave.

I run into what feels like a brick wall.

"What the fuck are you doing in my office?" Sebastian Blackwell booms.

I'm short, but I wish I were even shorter. I try to leave, but he blocks the exit and shuts the door.

Thunder explodes again outside, and I notice the lights everywhere in the building flicker and dim.

"Nothing," I finally say. "I was just leaving."

"I don't think so," Sebastian retorts. "You're not going anywhere. You've got some explaining to do. This is the second time you've been caught snooping in my office. I'm not going to ask you again, Brett. What the fuck are you doing in your boss's office?"

My palms sweat as I hear him shut the door behind me.

"I thought that…" I stammer, my words barely audible, and then I stop.

Holy fuck. Is it possible I am totally wrong and off base? That the reality where Mr X and Mr Blackwell are the same person is all in my head, a little fantasy of my own creation?

"Have a seat," Sebastian growls, his voice husky as he gestures to the chair in front of me. Nervously, I pull out my phone as he saunters slowly to the bar in his office. His suit coat is off and he wears a navy blue vest to go along with his pants. I stare at the man's frame from behind.

The white noise of the storm crashing against the glass window behind him is the only comforting sound in my environment.

Otherwise, I feel very much alone right now. I glance at the screen of my phone, and it goes dead. No service.

"Electricity is out in the town," Sebastian says, his back facing me while he pours a drink. "And the storm is supposed to last another three hours."

He spins around and our gazes meet. I wonder if he can sense my fear.

"Are you a whisky drinker, Brett?"

"That's what my daddy used to drink."

"I'll take that as a yes."

His steps are slow and methodical as he walks toward me, then hands me the drink.

"Thanks," I say, nervous as I look up at him.

"Cheers, Brett."

"Cheers," I return as we clink glasses.

"Let's get down to business, Brett."

"Let's," I squeak, my voice suddenly meek.

"You know I hired you because you are supremely talented. I can see that. Anyone can see that. And talent is just something you can't teach. It's like height. Either you have it or you don't. One of the main reasons I've been successful is my ability to spot talent."

"Thank you," I say.

He runs a hand through his hair, walks around to the other side of his desk, and sits with his hands folded.

"But the thing with talent, is that the most talented individuals are usually the most difficult to control. And it's evident that you do not give a shit about spending your time wisely at this job."

I shift my weight from side to side. "Um. Excuse me?"

Sebastian leans in, and licks his lips, like he's a lion about to pounce on his prey.

"I'm going to give you one chance to answer truthfully. What were you doing in my office?"

He takes a long sip of his whisky, sets the glass down and leans back, methodically examining me with his eyes, and flashing a cocky smirk.

I take a deep breath.

"I was looking for you," I breathe, and the possibilities flash through me of what this could lead to. Will he fire me?

Is there a chance that look in his eyes I've been sensing means the feeling is mutual?

"Why were you looking for me?"

I take a big, huge swig of my drink before I say what I'm about to.

"I needed to know if you're Mr. X. I want to know if you've been thinking about me...like that."

Without saying anything, Sebastian rises up from his

desk. I cross my legs and uncross them. I unfocus my eyes, in a sort of trance, until he reappears just in front of me.

"Do you like what Mr. X was saying?" He arches an eyebrow.

"I do," I mouth. "I want to get to know Mr. X. He's got a way with words...is that...you?"

"And *if* Mr. X were here, what would you want to do with him?"

He steps as close to me as he can. I stand up, and there are only inches between us.

"You want to fuck me. Don't you, Miss Blue?" he growls, cocking his chin back.

His words send a bolt of electricity through my body. Holy shit, he's crossing the line.

I lick my lips and whisper the only true word I can muster, "Yes." I nod

My heart pounds and my vision goes blurry. He takes my hand and guides me to his desk.

"Brett." He takes my hand. "I've been watching you for the past few weeks, and I want you. I want to get to know you more. I don't know what this is, but I need to find out more. Are you okay with that?"

"I'm okay with that."

"Alright. Good. Before we go any further. I'm going to need you to sign a NDA. This is ironclad. We will speak of none of this outside of you and I."

I hesitate for a moment, because this is happening so fast. Then again, a man like Sebastian probably can't take any risks.

"An NDA is fine with me," I say. "And actually, that's what I would prefer. I don't want to be that girl who 'slept her way to the top.' Whatever this is, we need to keep it between us."

I bend down to glance over the document. It appears to just be a standard NDA.

The pen shakes in my hand as I sign on the line, and when I'm done, I press my hand to his chest, almost involuntarily.

He grabs hold of my wrist and kisses me on the hand.

"Miss Blue. Or...should I call you Lacy?" He smiles.

He holds onto my waist through my skirt, and attacks me like a feral animal, pressing me into the cold glass window.

"Call me whatever you want," I mutter as he kisses my cheek, covering all of the surface area available.

He pulls back and runs a hand through my hair, grabs a fistful, and inhales. I smell him too, and his scent is musky and intoxicating. I run a hand on his cheek, feeling his five o'clock shadow.

The storm thunders outside, but it's nothing compared to the tornado that starts inside me when my boss pulls me to his body.

"Lacy. Brett. Miss Blue. I'm going to be honest--I don't give a fuck what your name is. I want to call you all three. I've been enamored with you ever since I laid eyes on you. I can't stop thinking about you. There's something about you. It's your spirit. It's your vibe. It's your goddamn scent--it's everything about you. I was already so physically attracted to you. And when I saw what you were writing--which is a whole other conversation we need to have, by the way--I couldn't help myself."

He runs his hand the length of my body, starting at the top of my back and working down to my hips, my ass, before landing his hand on the back of my thigh. "A girl as sexy as you shouldn't get to be as fucking smart and talented, too. It makes no sense, Lacy. You make no sense to me. No sense at all."

"And a guy as good-looking as you shouldn't also be the leader of a company. And an alright writer yourself. It makes no sense, Zane," I smile, saying his made up fantasy name. "No sense at all."

He kisses me once on the lips,

The rain pounds outside and the lightning flashes, but inside Sebastian's big arms I feel safe.

Inside, my heart pounds furiously, and I'm so glad it's sound drowned out by the thunder outside so he won't realize how much I want him in this moment. Maybe it's silly of me to try to cover up my desire in any way, but I can't help but think of that moment seven years ago when I caught him by surprise and kissed him.

Now, though I'm still his employee, all bets are off about how far we'll take things. I'm not just some sixteen-year-old girl with a fleeting crush.

We're both consenting adults, and I want to go all the way with him.

My breath hitches as I reach around and grab onto his ass, and the thing is just as hard as I thought it would be when I saw his buns in the shower. Dear God it's nice.

"Sebastian," I whisper as he works kisses down my neck. "I thought this would only be a fantasy. I never thought this would actually happen."

He runs the thumb and forefinger of his giant hand over my jaw, gripping me lightly.

"Well we're just getting started, honey."

"What are you going to do to me?"

His hand runs up my ass and finds its way under my shirt. He kisses his way down the side of my neck, then runs his tongue back up to my ear and whispers, "I'm going to make you mine. My little plaything. You want to write those little fantasies on company time? I'm going to give you something to write about."

"Oh God," I mutter, and run my hand down the outside of his vest, so aware of how hard his stomach is underneath his clothing. I move to untuck his shirt.

"Nah ah ah," he mouths, lightly but firmly gripping my wrist. "Hands off the merchandise." He smirks.

"You're truly an asshole, aren't you," I murmur.

"I am whatever you say I am. And I'm going to make you work for what you want. You've got a dirty mind, don't you, Miss Blue?"

"Yes," I admit.

"Say it, then. Tell me how dirty it really is."

"My mind is very dirty. So dirty."

"What do you think the rest of the employees at Blackwell Industries would think if they knew how fucking filthy the mind of the most innocent looking girl on the entire floor was?"

"I don't know," I whisper. "They'd probably be surprised. Are you surprised?"

His cheek brushes against mine as he growls in a low voice. "Are you asking if I'm surprised that the homegrown good girl tomboy of Blackwell has a filthy fucking mind? The answer is fuck yes. And after I'm done with you, it's going to be a whole lot filthier. You'll never be the same again."

My gaze drifts downward to his chest and forearms. Everything about the man is strength.

"Wha-what are you going to do with me?" I ask.

"All those fantasies you're writing? I'm going to turn them into reality. Every single one. So you just keep writing at your desk during work hours. And every day, I'm going to call you into my office. Or order you somewhere else in the building. I'm going to get creative. And I'm going to make all of the fantasies you write come true, Miss Blue. Every single fucking one. I'm going to make them come true, and then some. Now turn around."

When Sebastian came by my house weeks ago, I had no problem telling him off.

But right now, as his eyes sear into mine, his head slightly cocked, I'm on autopilot. I'm scared to think just how far I would go to please this man.

I do as I'm told. I turn around, forced to look at the dark, stormy weather outside. The rain pounds on the glass, and I can make out a partial reflection of Sebastian's menacing figure.

My heart pounds.

"Put your hands on the glass, sales girl," he snarls, and I palm the glass immediately. The flat surface is squeaky clean and cold on my hands.

"What are you going to do to me?" I ask. "I want to know."

He stands to the side of me and runs his hand through my hair. "I'm taking inventory of you. You're quite remarkable, Brett, have you ever realized that?"

"No."

He chuckles. "Suddenly you're so honest. I like it when you're honest. Well, since you haven't apparently realized it, I'm going to fill you in."

I let my head hang down, feeling suddenly incredibly vulnerable, and wondering what the hell I've gotten myself into.

"The first thing about you, Brett, is your smile. Every time I see it, it literally makes my day better."

I feel a gentle kiss on the cheek.

"Shall I continue?" he asks.

"Yes."

"I'm glad you want me to continue. Because I'm going to anyways. Your face and your hair are so gorgeous that it makes me suspicious when I talk to you, Brett. This blonde color, is it natural?" He fists my hair, and pulls it back.

"Yes," I mouth.

"Wow," he says. "Amazing."

"What's amazing? Why are you suspicious?"

"Brett, I'm amazed that a girl would have this much beauty and brains in one. Usually it's one or the other."

My heart skips a beat. "Oh," I say, and I don't expand on that, because I'm too shy to admit what I'm thinking to Sebastian.

But that's that best fucking compliment a man's ever given me.

"It's just...fuck, Brett. And the rest."

He runs a careful hand slowly down my spine, cups my ass, and then lands it between my thighs. Warmth rushes between my legs. I ache for him to reach just a bit higher on my body.

"It makes no sense, Brett. You make no sense. But..." he chuckles, and it's a natural laugh as if something catches him by surprise.

"What?" I ask, opening my eyes and turning my head toward him. "Why did you laugh?"

He rocks back on his heel, drink in one hand as he fixates on me. My mind goes to the worst place, and I wonder if this is all a big joke he's playing on me. Anger washes over my whole body, catching me by surprise, and I take my hands off the glass.

"Don't you fucking move," he says, and I freeze, but cross my arms and peer at him.

"I want to know why you laughed," I say again. "What are you hiding? Is this some kind of practical joke?"

"I wasn't laughing at you," he says. "I was laughing at how ridiculous my mind is. You ever have a voice inside you, something subconscious, that just forms a thought around something before you have time to filter it?"

"All the time," I admit.

"Yeah, well that happens to me a lot. And it just happened to you. Staring at you, running my hand over you, somewhere inside me I had the thought, 'you know, if a girl as beautiful as Brett Blue exists, there has to be a fucking God.'"

He smirks, takes another drink, and makes an 'ah' noise when he's done. My whole body heats up, and that's when I feel the space between us shrink, and my walls fall down. Somehow this man sees something in me no one else has ever grasped.

"Fuck, Sebastian. That's the nicest thing anyone has ever said to me."

In a moment he closes the physical space between us. "No one's ever told you how gorgeous and amazing you are? Don't lie now, Miss Blue."

I smile and look down. "They haven't put it like that."

"Well it's fucking true," he says before pulling me in for another kiss. "Now turn the fuck around so I can make you come."

I melt. It's his tone of voice, it's the things he says about me, it's his damn sexy body. It's the storm outside that makes me feel like we're in our own little bubble, away from the outside world.

I turn and he puts his hands on my hips from behind. I wonder what he'll do. "Take off those sexy white pants," he orders. "I want to watch you wiggle out of them."

I do as he says, first slipping off my shoes and then taking my pants off.

"Holy fuck. A thong."

I shrug and smile. "It's hard to find underwear to wear underneath white pants. Do you like it?"

"Like it? Brett, it's so damn hot."

"Really?" My skin tingles hearing Sebastian call me hot.

"Yeah. And you know what else is hot right now?"

"What's that?"

"You," he growls, and drops his hands to the flesh of my

hips. He kisses my neck from behind, and presses his hips into my ass.

"Holy shit," I breathe, able to feel the girth of his cock pressing into my ass through his pants. I reach clumsily behind me, trying to pet his hard length between his legs, but he grabs my hand.

"Nah-ah-ah," he whispers throatily. "Not yet. I have other plans in store for right now. Put your own hand between your legs."

He pulls my panties down to my knees, and I feel so awkward. Like this is all so unplanned and accidental.

I do as I'm told, because his voice has a hypnotic power over me. I lightly rub my middle finger over my already soaking clit.

"That's right," he whispers. "I want to make you come so hard, Brett. I do. God damn, you've no idea how much I'd love to just slide right in, feel this ass against my hips as I thrust deep inside you again and again. But you're not ready for that."

"I'm not?" I say, and the phrase comes out much more a question then I intended.

"You're not," he repeats firmly. "Not at all. But you're doing a good job yourself right now. I like how I can see your whole reflection in the window. God damn you're sexy, Brett. You know what, fuck it."

I moan loudly, the pleasure setting in.

I hear him unzip his pants and flop out his cock.

I glance down at it for just a moment and my jaw drops. "Massive," I manage to croak.

"Now hook two fingers inside yourself," he orders. "I want to see how you do it."

"Are you going to stroke yourself while you watch me?" I say as I do as he says, letting my fingers enter deeper inside me.

"Yes," he says. "I'm not going to fuck you yet, Brett. Even though I want to. Oh God, do I want to."

He steps to the side of me so I'm plainly in his view. It's the sexiest thing I've ever seen, my boss in a full suit with just his huge cock poking out as he stares at me with narrow eyes.

He doesn't say anything, but leans forward with his right hand, places it on top of mine on my pussy, collecting some of my juices. He brings the hand to his mouth, licks it, kisses me, and puts his two fingers in my mouth. I greedily suck, tasting myself, wanting, needing to feel him in any way he'll let me.

As I push deeper inside myself, I use my other arm against the window to still my balance. "Fuck Brett. So hot. So goddamn gorgeous in every way. I bet you'd love to feel this hard cock inside you, wouldn't you?"

"It's so perfect," I moan. "Your cock, I mean."

"I love when your voice is hoarse like that," he growls. "And yes. The cock gods have blessed me."

I want to laugh, but looking at him in the reflection, lightning flashing illuminating his handsome face, glancing back to his engorged cock --it's the hottest damn thing I've seen in my life.

I can't believe I'm about to come.

He slides back so he stands behind me, so close I can feel the warmth of his flesh almost touching my ass.

"That's right, Brett. Good girl," he says as he is vigorously pumping his shaft, watching me pleasure myself.

My body shakes, my knees quiver, and pleasure overtakes my entire body, bolts of warmth shooting to my limbs, filling my chest, and especially settling between my legs as I imagine him penetrating me.

"Oh fuck, it's hot when you moan like that. Oh fuck, your

ass is perfect. I'm so close, Brett. I haven't even touched you and you've got me so close."

"Come wherever you want," I blurt out.

He lets out a throaty noise halfway between a grunt and a shout. Placing the palm of his free hand firmly on the small of my back, he yanks up my shirt, exposing more flesh. Using the same hand, he tangles his left hand into my hair and pulls, forcing me to arch my back and press my ass against him.

Moments later I feel his cock touch my skin ever so slightly, and his warm cum spurts across my ass and lower back in thick rivulets, trickling down.

We both pant for a moment after, until he finally breaks the ice.

"Don't move," he says.

In the reflection of the glass, I see him move swiftly toward his desk and grab something.

"Workout towel," he explains as he helps wipe my back and ass clean. He wipes himself too.

"Aww, you're not even going to leave me any?" I joke. "I hear it's good for the skin. Got vitamin E or something."

He laughs, a strong belly laugh, different than I've ever heard him.

"I needed that."

"The orgasm or the laugh?" I ask, turning around.

He shrugs and pulls me in for a kiss, palming my ass cheek as he does. "Both." He leans in and kisses a spot just below my ear. "And you know what I need right now, since we aren't going anywhere?"

He nods outside, where the storm is still revving at full blast. Thunder rumbles through the muggy fall night.

"What do you need?" I ask, the possibilities seemingly endless.

"Another drink with you."

CHAPTER 13

ebastian

"You take anything with your whisky?"

"You have ginger?"

I smirk at her. "You *would* be a ginger girl."

I put some ice and whisky into both of our glasses, and some ginger ale into hers.

I hand Brett her drink, and we clink glasses as the rain hammers down outside.

"One of the worst storms I can remember in Blackwell," she says as she stares outside into the pitch black. I gaze outside, and I'm happy to take my mind off the fact that I just broke my cardinal, number one rule on which I built my business:

Never hook up with an employee.

"It's bad out there," I agree, letting my mind focus on the storm.

"I wonder if there's a tornado watch." Brett's eyes glisten in the dimmed light.

"Do you think I'd let us be on one of the top floors of Blackwell's tallest building if there was a tornado watch?"

I swagger toward my couch, because that's just how I feel after hooking up with the hottest, most precious girl I've ever seen.

Who would have suspected the most innocent looking one is the one with the dirtiest mind of all.

I bade her to come sit next to me on the leather couch, patting the spot next to me. "Come. Sit."

"I've already done the first, so I accept your proposal," she says, somehow with a straight face.

I throw my head back in laughter.

She sits next to me, and I run my eyes up and down her again.

"I feel a little ridiculous in no pants and a blouse," she says as she sits.

"Well you don't look ridiculous. You look fucking sexy."

"Really?"

She seems surprised, which shocks me.

"Hell yeah. Is the Pope Catholic? I'll answer that one for you. Yes, and you're sexy as fuck. Better get used to me saying that."

She chuckles, and runs her hand up my arm. Her touch gets my blood rushing.

I don't want this night to end. For most of the past year, life's been a slog of deals and plans and business wins and losses. Sure, I've had a few ladies thrown into the mix at times, but none like Brett.

I've never even had a shot at a wholesome-but-hot, sweet-but-naughty soul like Miss Brett Blue.

"Do you believe in fate, Brett?"

She leans her body into mine, and I wrap my arm around her.

Her face nuzzles into my shoulder, and she brings her eyes up. "Wow. You don't waste any time going deep, do you?"

I spin my glass of whisky and stroke her hair with my free arm. "I'm just curious about you. Us being reunited like this feels too big to be a coincidence. But I don't particularly believe in fate."

"So what do you believe?"

"I asked you first."

She takes a deep breath. "Fate and I are kind of at odds right now. My father died this year, and I'm trying to come to terms with why He would take my father away. It was too early. He was barely fifty."

She rubs her arm, and seems to tighten at the mention of her father. I hold her tighter, pulling her into me.

"I'm so sorry to hear that, Brett." I kiss her on the forehead.

"It's okay." She frowns. "I'm still processing it, though. I want to do right by him. It's why I didn't sell you the property."

"Because it reminds you of him?"

"He loved that damn house so much. His Dad--my grandfather--built it himself. I just can't part with it. Maybe someday. But not yet."

She smiles a little, and rests her chin on my shoulder, sitting up. "My father always told me to go after my dream. He worked hard so I could go to college, but I never got to finish."

She exhales deeply, blowing the air out of her lips like she's blowing out stress. Her eyes glassy, she looks off into the distance. For a moment, she closes her eyes and I swear I can feel her holding back tears.

"That's tough. Was going to college your dream?"

"It was for a while. But it was also my dream not to be in debt. So part of me gave up a little bit on that dream. And now--"

"You're just trying to live out your dream through writing a romance novel," I say, giving her the best shit-eating grin I can muster, trying to cheer her up a little.

"Stop it. You mean working for you, who for some reason thought I would be a good employee even though I have zero qualifications."

My arms still wrapped around her, I draw her into me on the couch. I love the feel of her flesh on mine. "You stop it. You have plenty of qualifications. You haven't even been on the job for a month and you're crushing it. Hell." I chuckle. "You're writing a damn romance novel on company time, and you're still more efficient than half my staff. And I've read it, Brett. It's fucking good."

She arches an eyebrow my way, her face so close I can feel her breath. "You're just saying that."

I shrug. "I'll admit I've never read a romance novel before. But I think it's fucking gold. It's got potential."

"I just wonder how it'll turn out in the end." She breathes, her mouth inches from mine.

I can't resist giving her a long, slow kiss. I nibble on her lower lip as I let go.

"You're the author. Don't you get to decide how it ends?"

The thunder booms loudly right outside, and she flinches, but I steady her.

"I have to let the characters tell me what they want to do." She smiles, and then sits back on the couch, grabbing her drink. "So, this fantasy thing we're doing. We're going to play one for me, and then one for you? Like I'll be Lacy, and you'll be Zane."

"I can be Zane. I always wished my name began with a 'Z' anyway."

"Alright. And you'll write something, then I'll write something. So we'll kind of cowrite the book."

I smile. "Of all the jobs I've had, I never thought I'd be cowriting a romance novel. I don't want any of the credit though, obviously. Just call me your secret ghostwriter. Deal?"

"Deal."

We shake on it.

This is going to be so much more than I bargained for when I hired her.

CHAPTER 14

rett

BRETT: *You're up early*
Mr. X: Same to you. 4 hours of sleep was enough?
Brett: The sleep I got on the couch was plenty. I had a very restful pillow
Mr. X: And I had a nice snuggle partner
Brett: Say snuggle partner again. That word is so funny
Mr. X: I'll give you something to snuggle with
Brett: Okay now that word is so dirty. You've ruined snuggle for me
Mr. X: I read what you wrote this morning. Looks like the creative juices are really flowing today
Brett: The earlier in the morning the dirtier I am
Mr. X: I'm still trying to process out how a girl as innocent looking as you comes up with these dirty thoughts
Brett: Never judge a book by its cover
Mr. X: Never again

Brett: So are you going to make this one happen? It's a challenging one

Mr. X: Do you doubt my superpowers? I only hope you'll be able to keep a straight face while you're doing it

Brett: So you're orally skilled is what you're saying

Mr. X: I'll let you be the judge of that. I can't wait to taste you

Brett: You got a taste last night

Mr. X: I need more

EARLY IN THE MORNING, Bob approaches my desk, and I quickly close the box with my conversation with Mr. X before my screen comes into view.

"Good Morning," I say in a cheery voice.

"Sounds like someone woke up on the right side of the bed today," he says quizzically.

I don't really want to tell Bob where I woke up--on Sebastian's office couch at two a.m. before we both groggily made it home.

I'm tired today, but it was certainly worth it for last night.

I shrug. "I sleep well when it rains. I've always liked the rain."

"Uh, okay. That's odd. Anyways, I got the email from the higher ups about your special role in the task force. I just wanted to say, anything you need, let me know what it is. I understand you'll be ducking out from time to time, and that's fine. What the bossman needs, he gets," he says. "And it sounds like he needs your help on this. I'm just surprised how quickly this all happened."

"Me too."

Bob passes by my desk and greets a few other employees, and I breathe a sigh of relief.

As I sip my morning coffee and peruse my morning emails, I respond to a few. I've been pulled off of the real estate sales team, and made a member of the design team, I'm cc'd on multiple emails coming through from my teammates.

Sebastian swears he can make any fantasy I want come true. Thanks to my creative mind, I'm not going to make this first one easy on him. I still wonder what he thought when he saw what I wrote this morning.

He's got to go down on me somewhere I'd never suspect it.

At eleven a.m., I report to the web-conferencing room where we're having the kick-off call with the design team. We're talking about getting the agreement finalized so the design team can work up their initial draft of the new ranch.

I'm surprised when I roll into an almost empty room, save for Troy. He's got his sleeves rolled up and his tie half undone.

"What's up killer?" He winks when I walk in.

"Where is everyone else?" I ask as I grab a seat.

He shrugs. "Some calls don't involve everyone, I guess." He connects a laptop to the hub in the middle of the big table. The big video screen directly in front of us populates, and a few moments later the image of a man and a woman appear.

"Hi!" They wave, and the woman speaks. "I'm Marsha and this is Frank." She nods. "We're your design team."

"Nice to meet you two," Troy says. "I'm Troy and this is my colleague Brett."

"Brett? Did I hear that right?"

The resolution is pretty good on the screen, and in the top right corner we can see a little icon of ourselves in the video screen.

"Yes, that's right. My name's Brett and I'm a girl. Let's get that out of the way first and foremost."

"Well alright then. Shall we get started?" Frank says.

We nod and I open my laptop to take notes. We talk about

the details of the ranch project. The designers are out of Austin, Texas, and although they are experienced in their profession, a ranch of this magnitude is not often designed, so the information I supply has more to do with the climate of Blackwell than anything else. When it rains, how cold it gets in the winter, things like that.

Fifteen minutes into the meeting, Fiona, the secretary, pops into the room.

"Oh excuse me. Sorry to interrupt. But Troy, you're needed in accounting. Big glitch. If you would."

She holds the door open.

"Think you can hold the fort down?" he says with a smug smile, nodding toward me.

"I can manage, thank you."

"Good. That's what I like to hear." He winks, pointing the laptop camera my way so I see myself in the upper right-hand corner. I lean forward on the table, the only thing visible is my upper body. Today I've worn a sleeveless dress, which showcases my arms that I've been oh-so-vigilant about working out in the gym.

I take a deep breath as Frank keeps talking about their process, and a feeling of accomplishment washes over me. I love this company, and I love the value I'm able to bring to it. In my early years of college, I never felt like I had a skill set that really served a purpose.

Sebastian Blackwell plucked me from the edge of oblivion, and thrusted me into a role where I contribute in a way that's perfect for my skill set.

I wonder if all that stuff he said last night was bullshit, or if I really make him believe there could be a God?

That comment went over my head at the time, but it's got to be the highest compliment anyone's ever given me in my entire life.

I smile softly, and Marsha's businesslike mood softens. I guess moods can be transferred digitally too.

"So then, the last thing we need to do is go through some of the design modules."

"Sounds good," I say, staring at the screen.

That's when Mr. X's name pops up on my laptop on the work messenger app.

Mr. X: Don't move, don't flinch, don't react

I furrow my brow. He shouldn't be contacting me during a meeting. Still, I answer back.

Brett: Excuse me?

Mr. X: it'll make sense in a minute

Brett: :thinking face:

Mr. X: I'm basically your genie. Your wish is my command. Loved what you wrote this morning. You're incredible

I FURROW my brow at the screen on my laptop, then look back to the big flat screen where Marsha and Frank are presenting.

"Is something...confusing?" Frank asks.

"No, no. Keep going," I say, motioning with my hands for him to continue.

The door opens and Sebastian enters, his dark brown eyes completely focused on mine as he steps in carefully, on the carpet. He notes the location of the flat panel TV, and strategically steps just to the side of the camera attached to the top.

Touching his finger to his lips, he motions for me to keep quiet.

I do my best to pretend not to notice him.

But even out of the corner of my eye, I can tell he's got a mischievous freaking look in his eye. He pulls out his phone, presses a button, and a song starts playing from his stereo.

My eyes go wide, and Frank's expression changes.

"Uh, is that "Motivation" by Kelly Rowland and Lil Wayne?"

"Yeah." I shrug, as if it's no big deal. "Our boss is trying a new productivity experiment. A study came out that employees are more productive while listening to music."

"Oh. Uh, okay. Anyways. This is a new and innovative design--it's never been done just like this to be honest. But I assure you the principles of design behind it are sound. Bear with me, since we still only have the designs on the physical board, I'll have to show you on the camera. It's a little old school, but it's the best way to show you."

Frank keeps talking, and I can barely keep a straight face.

Because my boss is standing just to the right of the flat screen, just barely out of view of the camera, doing a striptease.

To the beat of the music, he unbuttons one button at a time while making dead-on sex eyes at me. My heart pounds and my skin tingles, blood rushing between my legs.

Once his shirt is off, he does a belly roll, giving me the opportunity to see every single ripple of muscle in his abs.

I think back to the fantasy I wrote him this morning, and a rush of dopamine surges through as the realization hits me.

He's actually going to do what he said.

I know we agreed to this fantasy thing, but being honest, I didn't think he'd actually follow through. And what I wrote this morning was incredibly dirty.

Let's just say I have a history of men not following through and doing what they said they would.

After running his white dress shirt through his legs, he tosses it on the floor with the dirtiest, sexiest smirk I've ever seen.

I smile, and throw my head back in laughter.

But my jaw drops--literally--at what he does next.

He gets on his hands and knees, still avoiding the webcamera, and crawls underneath the table.

I swallow and my eyes go wide. "Holy shit," I whisper, and it's too late when I realize I've whispered the words out loud.

"You like it that much?" Marsha asks, raising an eyebrow.

"Yes," I choke, trying to stay focused on the task at hand. "It's very impressive."

"Thanks. The new gutter feature is especially designed for the stormy weather of Blackwell. It'll keep the cows from getting wet." She winks.

I flinch at first when I feel him touch my legs.

I feel soft kisses start at my ankles as Sebastian works his mouth up the insides of my calves and thighs. His touch is delicate as his tongue licks and caresses me while I try not to move a muscle. I need to keep my poker face for the conference call. Above the table, business decorum is observed and Frank and Marsha continue their presentation. I just smile and nod, because the above the table action is not what I care about right now.

Since below the table, out of sight of the glaring, judgmental eye of the public is where my fantasies come true.

His kisses and licks dangerously close to my mound, and I move my legs wider apart, for him. I feel the heat of his breath and the strength of his fingers on my legs as his face arrives between my legs.

"No panties," he says, hesitating before he touches me. "Just as I asked. Here's your reward for being such a good girl."

He flicks his tongue on my clit and I squirm in pleasure. In my image in the upper right-hand corner of the screen I watch as my own face turns as red as a ripe apple.

He licks again, working his tongue on my clit.

He's probably loving torturing me, having his way with me in a public forum like this. For me, the real torture is not being able to moan as loud as I want. I'm not allowed to thread my fingers through his hair or cry out his name and beg him not to stop.

I sink lower into my chair and I resist him as best I can. This was the fantasy I wrote but that doesn't mean it was meant to come true.

Does it?

Holy fuck, what's he doing, tornados with his tongue?

I swallow and place my hands flat on the table, hanging on for dear life.

"As you see, it's a prototype and we can alter the design, but it's engineered exactly to Mr. Blackwell's specifications. Have you seen Mr. Blackwell by the way? He seemed so sure he would come to this meeting."

"Coming?" I repeat, my eyes hazy with pleasure. "Not yet. It feels good though. So good."

I clasped my hand over my mouth, realizing the words I just said.

"Feels...good?" Marsha asks.

"Yes," I fumble, and that asshole licks my pussy harder. I can't fucking think. "I mean I'm not a design expert but Mr. Blackwell told me the 'feel' of the design and this feels good so to speak. Oh fuck it feels so good!"

Uh oh. I see the shocked looks on the faces of Marsha and Frank. They must think I'm a crazy person. "Thank you, Marsha," I manage to say. "I mean the design--it's got a good feel to it. I think the "feel" is really important. Don't you?"

I let out a loud, awkward laugh, and Marsha, gives me sort of a funny look, but continues explaining the ins and outs of the design. Personally, I'm going to have to watch this presentation on playback, because the real show—speaking of ins and outs—is going on right now below the table as Sebastian dips two fingers inside me to go along with his tongue.

I strain in vain not to let the pleasure be evident on my face, but it's too great. This feels so wrong, but I can't help but let go as Sebastian takes me to the brink. My core warms, my legs tingle, my spine tingles. Electricity spurts through me. My toes curl, my calves tense.

I hope to God the webcam microphone isn't so sensitive it picks up every last detail of the audio. I'm breathing way too hard for a boring conference call. My breath hitches and waves of pleasure crash through me as I come.

This is no ordinary orgasm. This orgasm feels like it was prepared on a platter, served to me—a fine dining meal, prepared by my fucking billionaire boss. What possessed him to actually follow through on this promise, to make the fantasy I wrote this morning come true, I still don't quite understand. Another thing I don't quite understand is where these dirty thoughts and idea of mine come from. As I come down from my orgasm, he softens his touch. And I recall, what Sebastian mentioned yesterday about his subconscious, where he believes most of his thoughts rose from.

As I stare at Frank and Marsha, who are still pointing and talking about the project, my mind wanders. My thought is fleeting, but it's there. And it's the happiest thing I'd ever conceived. I don't know why my strange mind takes this sort of lesson away from my boss and then down on me. But I think to myself, if this fantasy about my boss pleasuring me in a public setting can come true, then what *can't* I do? It's a powerful feeling to believe that your mind has a capability of lurid wishes come true. Even sexual fantasies, design plans, or otherwise, maybe Sebastian understands what it means to have dreams and follow through on them.

And that's why he wants to make all my fantasies come true.

Though I have my doubts that Sebastian's thought this

deeply about what one orgasm like this can do to a girl like me.

As he pulls away from my clit, I take a deep breath, just let myself be, just exist. Sebastian is the kind of man that doesn't talk about doing, or write about doing. He *does*. Period. He takes swift action when he wants something, and that's why he's so rich. Probably also why I'm so damn attracted to him, period. He pulls away completely, and I'm left with a feeling of emptiness without him touching me.

When he reappears just outside of the line of site of the web camera, he grabs his shirt just to the left, puts it on, button by button, while he stares at me with his sex glare. His face is the cockiest, sexiest gesture a man's ever made to me. He rubs his forearm, he rubs his mouth with his forearm, wiping his face clean of my juices. I damn near have another orgasm just from the sight.

I zone back in to Marsha, who is tapping her microphone.

"Are you still there? Is this still working?"

"Oh, yes," I say. "I was just thinking how amazing it is that you, Mr. Blackwell, everyone, that were all able to take our shared vision, and make it into reality. It's truly incredible."

"Wooh, okay!" she says. "Glad to hear that! I was getting a little bit nervous there when you weren't saying anything.

"Yep, well, it's all good," I say. "Nicely done!"

Sebastian opens the door, and shuts it loudly, pretending that he's entering the room.

"Heyyy, Frank! Marsha! So sorry I'm late. I meant to make this meeting."

Frank chides him. "We were kind of lucky to have Brett here. She can give you a summary of what was talked about."

"What meeting was so important that you had to ditch us?" Marsha asks with a wink.

"Well, I kind of had an impromptu late lunch," he says with a giant smirk, and looks me dead in the eye.

I about die.

He grabs a seat in the chair next to me. "Hey, Brett, actually, can you check and make sure I don't have anything in my teeth? Look," he says, smiling his pearly whites at me.

"Well, anyways, we've got to jet," Frank says. "We've got another call at around 11:30, but let us know if you have more questions."

"Adios." Sebastian nods, and mercifully, the video cam cuts out.

"Oh my God. You are insane!" I say.

"Yep!" is all Sebastian says as he wiggles his eyebrows and leans back in his chair.

"They've been telling me I was insane ever since I was dirt poor, and said I was going to become a millionaire. Anything else you'd like to report?"

"Yeah, on Thursday, it's my turn. I get to call the shots, unless you want to back out, which is fine."

I scrunch up my brow at him. "What, you don't think I can handle your fantasy? No, I'm not backing out, alright? Thank you."

He smirks. "I'll have it ready--I mean, my alter-ego *Mr. X* -- will have the fantasy ready for you when you come in. Now, if you'll excuse me, I actually do need to get to my second lunch for today. Don't worry, this is an actual lunch, that wasn't a sexual comment or anything."

I laugh. "Get out of here!" I say, pushing his shoulder playfully.

And he goes.

CHAPTER 15

rett

THE NEXT DAY IS SATURDAY, and I take a much needed breather from work to take my sister to her soccer game. My sister Macy is fourteen, and in the car she's peppering me with questions about the new job.

"So you're seriously working at Blackwell Industries?" she asks.

"Uhh, yeah," I say.

"How did you get that job?" I explained to her how I turned Sebastian down, and that made him think I would be a good fit.

Macy nods, processing this information.

"So, you're saying I should shut down the guys I like and they'll want me?"

I chuckle. "I don't know if that will always work. But you could try it, I guess. Although I don't know if guys your age will be able to handle that kind of rejection."

"Oh, King can definitely handle it. He's the captain of the football team. He's used to that kind of thing."

"So this King guy is the one you have a crush on?"

"Uh, yeah! He's the guy everybody likes. I don't think he likes soccer girls though. Apparently, he has a thing for gymnastics girls."

I glance over at Macy. She's gorgeous. Fourteen, brunette. Her eyes are hazel, and looking at her makes me think I got the short end of the stick when it comes to looks in our family. And for her to think she's anything else aside from damn gorgeous hurts my heart.

"Macy, you're a catch," I say.

She laughs, looks over at me.

"*You're* a catch!"

She rolls her eyes. "Thanks, Sis. Changing the subject, what's this I hear about you writing a romance novel?"

My grip on the steering wheel tightens.

"A romance novel?"

She smiles, like she's got the dirty on me.

And she does. Not like I would keep something from her intentionally, but she's young.

"*Yeah*, I know about that," she continues. "Crystal's sister told me Crystal talked to her sister, her sister talked to me. I'm actually a little bit upset that you don't trust me enough to tell me."

"Okay, you got me. I'm writing a little story for fun. Don't take it personally that I didn't tell you. Of course I trust you. But I don't know if I'm a good writer. I don't tell a lot of people about it. You obviously know how."

"I do know. And I'm curious. Where do you get your inspiration? You haven't dated in like forever. Since who, Patrick?"

"You mean the one who shall not be named." I chuckle,

and luckily we are pulling up to the Blackwell High School parking lot so we can end this awkwardness.

"Have a good game, kid."

"I'm not done grilling you on this," she says as she jumps out and grabs her gear from the back of the car. "I need to know all about this book."

I park and head out to the Blackwell High School stadium, where the JV team has just taken the field. Macy goes with the varsity squad and does warm-up drills in the adjacent field.

I watch the game and enjoy the gorgeous fall weather.

Right before the varsity game starts, there's a special announcement at midfield.

The head coach gets on the microphone, standing next to some Booster Club members and a few other people.

And then Sebastian Blackwell walks out, to whistles from the girls and cheers from the parents in the stands.

The coach says a few words. "And big thanks to the patron who made this new field possible, Sebastian Blackwell. We wouldn't have been able to make this happen without your generous donation, and we'd like to present you with a special dedication."

A few of the girls step forward with a golden plaque and ceremoniously hand it over to Sebastian. He steps to the podium.

"Yeah, I just want to thank all the teachers and the coaches I had during my time in Blackwell, who taught me all the lessons that I needed to be successful in life. They taught me that if I want something, all I need to do is go after it and work hard for it. As long as we have the right people and the right team in place, there is nothing we can't achieve." He speaks loudly, deeply, and from the heart. The crowd is riveted. He turns toward the line of girl soccer players standing on the sidelines. "And kids, I want you to know I was once standing in your shoes too. The most important lesson you need to take is that if your mind can conceive and believe something, you can achieve it. Now let's have a good game!"

The crowd roars and Sebastian waves as he leaves the field.

My heart warms, and a new version of Sebastian takes hold in my heart.

One who is capable of loving as well as he does...other things.

Things that involve his dexterous tongue.

The field is incredibly nice, especially for a town like Blackwell, that hasn't got the most attention in terms of funds over the last few decades. We've been a pass-over town in so many ways.

I poke the soccer moms sitting on the bleacher next to me on the shoulder, because I'm curious about something.

"Hey, excuse me. Do you know how much this field cost?"

"Yeah, actually" she says. "I was on the committee that helped fund it. It was around five million dollars after everything."

"Five million? Oh my God."

"Yes," she beams. "Five. I know a lot of people don't like him, but Mr. Blackwell's a generous man."

I watch as Sebastian, now standing on the sideline and watching the beginning of the game, scans the crowd. We make eye contact, and he furrows his brow in the sun.

He says something to the head coach, and then makes a beeline toward me.

"Oh my God!" the soccer mom says. "Is Sebastian Blackwell coming our way?"

"Uh, yeah," I say. "Hm, he's really a man of the people."

He's trying not to walk toward me with a giant smile on his face.

"Hi," Sebastian says simply when he arrives to our spot in the bleachers. He smiles at me, then, reaches out a hand for the woman next to me. "I'm Sebastian."

"I know who you are," she says, blushing. "I'm Samantha."

The way she speaks, there's a clear subtext. *I'm Samantha and I'd love to get to know you a little more.*

"The sky's so damn blue today." He smiles, ignoring her flirty look. "Can't think of many things out there as blue as this damn sky."

He looks me dead in the eye, and I can't help but recall what he said about my eyes. "Mind if I take a seat?" he asks.

"Uh, sure!" Samantha says lickety-split, maybe a little too fast to my liking.

Am I getting jealous of this woman?

I watch her line of vision as she stares him down in Saturday clothes. Sebastian looks so much different than how he appears in the office. He's got on jeans, boots, aviator sunglasses, and a t-shirt. If I didn't know any better, I would have thought it was just some sexy cowboy.

He sits right between the two of us, and Samantha does a good job of giving him just enough room so that he's forced to graze her thigh. "I tell you what," he says. "Days like these I live for. Sun in my eyes. People playing sports. Having a good time. Reminds me of my own high school sport days. And these kids out there, they are just living the damn dream."

He scrubs a hand across his jaw, and shoots me a secretive, knowing smirk that sends goose bumps through me.

I decide to put in my own two sense into the conversation.

"It makes me think of what I've always said. If you can make your dream into reality, or your fantasy to reality… that's what life is for."

Sebastian shoots me a funny look, squinting through the sun. "Since when do you always say that?"

I smile, my leg just an inch to the right. Our legs are touching.

"Since yesterday," I say with a peculiar smile. "I had a special lunch meeting with my boss. It made me realize a few things."

"Oh," Sebastian says. "That sounds like a successful lunch out."

"I'm sorry," Samantha interjects. "Where do you work again?"

"I work at Blackwell Industries." I can't help the devilish grin that spreads across my face.

"Uh, alright…so you two know each other."

I shrug. "You could say that."

Sebastian and I exchange a knowing glance, and I feel good that we share a secret.

We settle into the action of the game, and make small talk. Macy scores a goal and we cheer her on. When it's all over, Sebastian stands up. "Well ladies, it's been a pleasure, but I've got to be going."

"Bye," I say, and resist winking.

Samantha stands up as well, and hugs him goodbye. "Such a pleasure to meet you. I do have a small arts and crafts business, so let me know if you want to hang out and um, talk *business*."

The way she says business makes me think she wants to do anything but.

I want to kiss him and show how I'm his, how he's taken, but I freeze up. I can't do anything. Our relationship isn't official. It's nothing.

As he walks away, I watch him. We're not built to last. Our relationship, if you can call it that, is a shooting star bound to flame fast and die hard. I might as well not get emotionally invested, especially if that's not something Sebastian wants.

Of course I'd want something more with him. But for now, I'm just going to enjoy the ride he's taking me on.

He looks damn good in those jeans. His normal workday clothes don't do Sebastian's ass justice. As a matter of fact, I think I have my inspiration for my next scene with Lacy and Zane.

CHAPTER 16

ebastian

THE WEEKEND FEELS like it takes forever. All I do is think about Brett and what I'm going to write for her on Monday.

I arrive early to work, and type a scene up for Lacy and Zane.

It's something I've been wanting. Wishing I could do for a long time, but not just with anyone. It had to be the right girl.

Brett is that girl.

Once I get started writing the scene for Lacy and Zane, the words flow easily.

Let's just say this one involves a bottle of tequila, a striptease, and a late night at the office.

By the time I'm done writing it, my cock is a steel rod, and I've got to do a round of pushups and pull ups to get rid of it.

I hit 'send' on the attachment to Brett's personal inbox from my alias gmail inbox, Mr. X.

Hey, it's a little corny to have an alias, but I can't have a digital trail leading back to me. I'm sure there are hackers who would love to get a billionaire's secret love life in their hands.

Later that morning, I do something I haven't done in quite some time.

I call my Dad.

I'm not sure exactly what inspires me to do this. But I have a vague feeling of warmth still spreading through my heart after sitting with Brett and watching her sister play soccer last Saturday.

"Hello?" His gruff voice picks up after two rings. "Who's this? I don't want any sales calls. My wife and I have a fine sex life. We don't need any pills."

"Dad, it's me." I laugh.

"Liam?"

"No, it's your other son." I lean back in my chair. This is one of my Dad's favorite games to play with me. He's never let go that I didn't take on the family business. "I know, it's been a while."

"I'm just fucking with you, kid! I know. You never call me though. So what do I owe this pleasure?"

"I just wanted to ask how are things going on the farm these days."

"Well, harvest this year ain't the worst, but I'm not complaining. I've got a roof over my head. But seriously... what are you calling me about? You feeling guilty about something? Some other way I fucked up raising you you wanted to mention to me?"

"Have no reason Dad, I just wanted to see how you were doing."

There's a long pause of silence before he finally speaks. "You just wanted to see how I was doing on a Monday morning. Well, hell."

"Yeah, I wanted to give my dad a call, what's wrong with that?"

He lets out a huff. "Look, I'm not going to sit here and act like I'm not surprised that's all. You never call me." I take a deep breath.

What am I to say to this guy? My father knows I haven't been the best at keeping up with him, what with how focused on work I've been over the last decade. I've let our relationship go. And now for some odd reason, seeing a girl that I have a crush on has led me to want to give him a call just out of the blue.

But I don't say any of that.

"Dad, I wanted to see if you want to go golfing this weekend."

"Golfing!"

"Yeah. I was thinking you, me, and Liam could go out and, you know hit the greens for a hot eighteen. Drink some beers."

"Hell, I'm open next Sunday. Plus, that's the Lord's day so I might as well."

"Sounds good, Dad. We'll just see you then. I'll let Liam know."

I hang up the phone and I feel good. Surprisingly good just for a simple call to my Dad.

THAT NIGHT I stay late in the office. I watch the sunset and then some. In fact, I go get my workout in and then two hours later I'm still in the office. I glance up when there's a knock at the door. My heart hammers, because who the fuck would be coming in here at this hour? And then my brain jolts awake. I really spaced out that hard.

I know exactly who it's going to be.

Brett enters, strutting sexily toward me.

"Mr. Blackwell. I was staying late and I thought I would come in and see how you were doing."

The tone of her voice is laced with sex and seduction.

Fuck, she looks sexy in just her regular work clothes from today. She's got on tight blue pants and a scoop neck shirt that puts her boobs on good display. I stand up to greet her. It's been a stressful day.

"I'm doing better now that you're here." I exhale. "I was just putting some fires out with the new distillery.

"Oh," she says, looking down at my desk. "Did they fuck something else up?"

I laugh. "Not yet but that's what I'm trying to avoid."

She walks to the bar in my office and goes straight for the bottle of tequila. Holy shit. She's doing it. I can't believe she would follow through.

"Tequila in the office?"

She tilts her head slightly toward me. "Yeah, I have no idea where I got the idea. Must have been something that seeped into my subconscious. It's not like I read a story about this or anything." Her tone is laced with sarcasm.

I squint my eyes as if I'm confused. "Yeah, that's totally odd." I chuckle, and so does she. Her body language relaxes a little.

"To be honest I thought you were out. I didn't think you would want to keep up this little game we have going. I don't know. Something just told me you were becoming impatient or fed up with my ways."

"Not sure where you would have gotten that impression. By the way, it was good to see you last Saturday."

"I thought it was quite the surprise. I didn't even know you had a sister."

"And I didn't know you were a fan of donating so much of your money to causes.

"There's a lot you don't know about me."

"Touché." I wink.

She rolls her eyes. "Do you think we'll ever…" her voice trails off. "Forget it."

There's a touch of sadness.

"Think we'll ever what?"

She shrugs. "It doesn't matter."

I stand up, walk toward her, and put my hand on her shoulder. "You okay? You seem off. And if you're thinking something, it *matters*."

"Yeah," she says, looking down and away. "I'm totally fine. I'm great."

"Really? Because you don't look fine."

She takes a deep breath. "I really am fine. I just had a hard day working."

"Tell me about it."

Her blue eyes narrow and as she looks up at me. "How do you do it, Sebastian? I mean I've only been here for a few weeks and I'm already stressed out. You're here like it's nothing on a Monday night! Don't you have a family, friends that you want to be with?"

I take a deep breath because she's right.

"I have sacrificed a lot to get to where I am with this job at this company; my company. And I think sometimes about what could have been, but then I just try to push the thought out of my head and not think too much about it. Because if I do then I stop working. I just try to stay in motion."

She nods, then hands me a glass of tequila on the rocks with a little bit of lime, just the way I wrote it this morning. I grip the cold glass but don't sip it yet. "Well I would love to be able to make all your problems go away at least for a little bit."

"You already have," I say. "The moment you walked in that door, I couldn't think of anything besides you."

She laughs. "Really?"

"It's the truth. Isn't that ridiculous? Brett, you look sexy as fuck just in your regular work clothes. I almost want to change what I wrote this morning. Just take those off and ravish you right here. But I also want to savor this night, if we're doing...everything I wrote."

"I almost want you to just rip these off me too," she admits. "But I went all the way to Victoria Secret during my lunch break to find the appropriate color...for Lacy. And we are damn well going to follow through on this."

I laugh. "The things you do for me."

She shakes her head.

"I know, I think I'm insane sometimes. So I think this is what we're going to do." She holds up her glass, and we stare at each other, enthrallingly. We hesitate for a moment, both taking swigs of our tequila. Our eyes lock again and I lean in for the kiss.

Forget sugar and spice and everything nice. She tastes like sex and tequila and everything filthy.

I dim the lights, sit down on this couch and that's how we start.

She flashes a smile, her hand dipping to my ribcage. She loves my damn abs, doesn't she? Feeling her touch, all the time I've spent in the gym pays off; knowing how she melts in my arms. The lights are dim and I can barely make out her face, her cheeks, all of her loveliness. She's an angel sent just for me. As I try to comprehend why Brett Blue was put into my life, I don't fucking know. It makes no sense. To be honest, if we're talking karma here, I think I've always been kind of a dick. So maybe in some past life I did something else to deserve this.

"Close your eyes," she whispers.

I do, and I hear her fumbling with her phone.

She puts on a song, and I'm so impressed by her attention

to detail because it's the same song I wrote to her in my twisted fantasy this morning.

"Tequila Makes Her Clothes Fall Off" by Joe Nichols plays, and I hear her walk back toward me on the couch.

I sink into the cushions, enjoying the smell of her.

"Okay Sebastian," she says. "Open your eyes.

My jaw drops. "Fuck you're sexy," I blurt out, but words don't do her justice.

Her pants are off, neon yellow bottoms hugging her hips, complemented by a lace bra-top of the same color. It's not the easiest song to dance to, but she pulls it off, tossing her hair around and swaying to the song in such a way that turns my cock right into a steel rod.

"So I have to ask." She smiles. "What's this thing with this color? Neon yellow? Seems weird."

I shrug. "No reason. I just like it. It goes well with tequila."

"You are indeed a simple man. That's it. There's no weird story behind this."

"Why can't a man just like a color?" I smirk. "It pleases me. Although trust me, the color is not the sexiest thing about this scene right now."

"Oh, what is?" she asks, taking another sip of her drink.

"That would be you."

"Oh."

She dances as the song winds down, and she picks up her phone.

"Take off your shirt," she says. "You need some music to do it?"

"I can take off more than just my shirt," I say. I stand up and take off my shoes, my socks, my slacks, letting her watch me. Before I sit back down I offer a confession.

"I thought about you this weekend," I say. I reach for my drink on the coffee table, take a strong sip, then go back to the bar to refill. "Like before I even saw you on Saturday."

I was thinking about you too," she offers, but doesn't elaborate. "I was thinking about what happened on Friday to be honest."

"It was hot." I say. "I've never done anything like that. Do you need a refill?"

"I'll take a little more."

I give her a quick top off, and squeeze a little lime in her glass.

"I couldn't believe the look on that soccer mom's face when you told her you went out to lunch. You're a dick."

"I like to have a little fun. What can I say?"

"I don't see anything wrong with that." I take another step toward her. I grip her head, pull her into me and plant another kiss on her lips.

"That whole thing was just so ridiculous," she said. "You're so ballsy, but I got a strange lesson out of that."

"You got a lesson from me going down on you?" I say, curious.

"It's totally silly and I was probably reading more into it more than I should have, but yes I did."

"And what was the lesson that you got out of it?"

"I don't want to talk about lessons right now I just want…"

I let my hand drift down to her ass and grab it.

"This," she whispers, gripping my hand and pressing me further into her.

She moans, backing up.

"You really want to. You want to have sex with me. Right now."

"I do, I, God I really do," she purrs, and I can see the truth in her eyes.

Our foreheads touch and she runs her hand from my chest down to my abs.

"I'm a little bit scared if I'm being honest," she says.

"God. I want you so much. I've wanted you for a long time. Longer than the last three weeks," I say.

"Yeah," she admits, "I've wanted you since I knew you as the owner of the pizzeria back in the day."

My heart hammers. "You, wow, I didn't think you were old enough to think about those things, but I can see that..."

"Hey, don't act like you're so much older than me. You're only seven years older."

"Seven or six, whatever. How old are you?

"I'm twenty-three."

"Oh," I say. "I'm twenty-nine. So six years older."

"You act like I'm a little girl. I'm twenty-three."

I sigh. "I don't mean it like that. You're amazing but fuck it--I want this."

"And I want to give it to you," she says.

"I fucking know you do but," my tone is joking, but cocky. "Do you think you can handle this?" I grip her hand and bring it down to my cock.

I inhale her air, kiss down to her ear, and whisper, "Don't worry, you'll always make room for me. I know you can."

"I'm so wet right now," she whispers back. I let my hand drift between her legs.

"Fuck baby, you're soaked. You're going to soak right through these yellow panties, aren't you?"

"I already have," she purrs. "So why don't you let me get another song going and I'll make this happen. This is our first time and I want it to be amazing."

She pushes me back onto the couch. Well she pushes me and I voluntarily sit on the couch and I watch her, fascinated. She grabs her phone from her pocket and puts on a song. It's a slow acoustic.

"What is this?" I ask.

"It's one of my favorites, "Meant to Be."

I love the feeling, the moment, everything just washes over me about what we're doing.

It just feels so damn *wrong* that my employee can make me feel this way.

But we've shattered the employee-employer barrier, and she's rapidly on her way to getting many more benefits than just her 401k.

It's a soft acoustic song but a sweet song, and it will never have the same meaning for me again. Brett smiles and does a little dance, swaying her hips to the beat of the song but keeping her eyes on me. God, she's sexy. She's temptation. She runs her hands through her hair, squeezes her tits together, and loses herself in the dance. Spinning around, she shakes her ass, moving closer to me. I'm no Neanderthal, but all of the available blood in my body has now rushed to my cock, and I'm sure feeling like one. Turning back to face me, Brett bends over to give me a close-up of her tits before she undoes her bra.

Sitting on my lap, she wraps the lace of her bra around my neck.

"Don't move," she whispers, devilishly. I want so badly to reach out and just take her, but I also want to see where she's going with this. With her soft lips, she runs soft kisses down the side of my neck.

"Holy shit," I groan as she grinds against me.

"You like the striptease?" she asks.

"Fuck yeah, I do."

Still, even when she's doing a sexy dance for me, somehow the girl manages to convey that everlasting innocence of hers. It's hard to have a coherent thought about a girl this smart, this sexy. She's like my Lois Lane--an unsuspecting, bookish girl by day, and a sexy stripper by night.

My own personal sexy stripper.

"Brett..." I say, my voice husky.

She opens her eyes, stares at me for a moment, and stands up. Turning around, she bends over to get her cocktail, teasing the fuck out of me.

"Yes, Boss?"

I take a sip of my tequila. "You make no fucking sense to me."

"I make no sense? What do you mean?"

I lean back in my chair, and though I've got the tequila in my hand, it's her I'm drinking in. Her blonde hair falls to her shoulders, framing her beautiful red lips and smile. I have to remind myself this is real life.

"Your existence perplexes me. It's amazing."

"You're as weird as I am." She giggles. "A total weirdo. I think it's one of the reasons I'm so comfortable around you."

"Are you weird?" I ask. She takes a few steps toward me.

"Oh, I don't know. I'm just exchanging sex letters with my boss that are loosely part of a romance novel I'm writing, and now I'm about to sleep with him. So sure, I'm a little weird."

"Are you really? You're about to sleep with your boss?" I tip my chin back.

"Yes," she says, her voice a whisper, and it's the sweetest 'yes' I've ever heard.

"Hey." I reach my hand up and it touches her chin. She's gotten so close to me. The striptease already has me hard as hell but I need to ask her this before I go way over the edge here.

"From here, Brett, there's no going back and I need to know that you're okay with this. I'm asking you person to person. Is this what you want?" I see it in her eyes. I know the answer before it comes out of her lips but it sounds so sweet when she says it.

"I want you so bad. Sebastian, I've wanted you for…just fuck me already, will you? You've asked me enough. Just take me. I'm yours, and this isn't me acting out some silly fantasy.

This is what I want. You." Her tone is irritated. Impatient. She wants this as badly as I do.

"Fuck, that's hot to hear you say that. Because you're what I want, too. So much."

I grip her hips and guide her onto me so that she's straddling my waist on the couch. My hard dick pokes almost through my briefs into her panties. We make out furiously and this time it's different. We grind against each other. This time it's going to end in a way that will satisfy us both. I mean not that going down on her the other day wasn't totally satisfying. But this time we can both feel that it's on.

It's so fucking on.

"Wait." She moans. "Put your hands behind your back." she says.

Fuck! I forgot I wrote about that this morning; even though I wrote about her teasing me, now all I want is to be inside of her right now but she delays my gratification. She pulls off my briefs and then keeps dancing with the music. Throwing her hair around, she bounces her hips from side to side. She even twerks a little bit at me and I'm about to lose it.

"You're so fucking hot right now. You have no idea." She turns around, bends down, and comes oh so close to kissing my cock but she doesn't. She just blows on it. "God damn you're a fucking tease," I say. She stands up and spins around, and her ass facing me, she pulls down her panties and dropping them around her ankles.

"I'll show you a fucking tease," she says. She turns around and I don't care where she told me to put my hands. I slip them around and grab her tits as I make out furiously with her.

"Brett, I need to be inside you right fucking now."

"Okay," she finally says. She straddles me on the couch and eases onto me, taking my tip in first. She's wet but she's tight and I've still got to work to get inside her. She bounces up and down for a time, for a few moments just on the first inch or so on my cock until she is able to get the whole thing inside. When she does she lets out the hottest moan I've ever heard in my life.

"Mmm, oh my God. Sebastian."

"Fuck me, Brett." I say. I grab the back of her neck. Spread kisses all over her breasts.

"Okay," she says "Fuck you? I can do that now."

She begins to bounce very slowly up and down riding the length of my cock. She's so tight and slick, she feels amazing but it's more than that. It's that it's her and that's when I know she's the one for me. There's something about her scent and still while she grinds her hips against me I feel like I'm fucking an innocent girl, that she's my innocent girl. I love that she shows this side just to me.

The very first time you're fucking someone is in a way a strange time to realize that you're probably in love with someone but for me if I'm being honest, that's how it goes down. I want to just tell her right there, but the thought is fleeting. A few moments later all I can think about are Brett's eyes as I stare into them. She closes them and I grip her hair, grip her head and point it at me.

"Brett, open your eyes," I growl.

"Sebastian," she moans, and lets her eyes drift open.

She lets out another moan and tonight I hear the soft drizzle of a Blackwell rain shower drifting against the window. Very different from the thunderstorm the other night. Tonight we're the thunderstorm and for the next, oh I don't know--one, two, three, four, five, ten, twenty minutes-- we fuck. We fuck like animals. We fuck like thirsty desert goers, who haven't been exposed to food or drink for many days, weeks--hell maybe even years--because that's how long it's been since I felt this way about someone.

She straddles me as I sit on the couch, I love watching her face bobbing in pleasure.

"Do you like that, Brett?" I whisper, pulling her into me. "Do you like feeling your boss's cock deep inside you?"

Breathing hard, she nods.

"Say it. I want you to tell me what you like."

"I like feeling your cock deep inside me," she mouths.

"Good girl. And I love the way you grip me with your pussy." I grip her ass with my hand, guiding her hips up and down on my cock.

After who knows how long, we get up. She sits back on the couch, panting, her legs wide open.

I dive between her legs, flicking her clit with my tongue. I want her taste, and I want to hear her moans.

God damn, do I want to hear her soft moans.

"Oh God," she breathes, digging her nails into the cushions behind her.

I pull up for a moment. "I like it when you say my name." I smirk.

"I didn't say your name though. I said, 'oh God.'"

"That's right." I smirk.

"You cocky bastard," she mewls.

I turn her body around and we go at it doggy style.

We're a sweaty mess of arms and limbs and parts and pleasure.

The slap slap slap of my hips against her ass, that sweaty skin on skin sound, reverberates through the room.

"Oh God, you're going so deep," she whimpers, her voice music to my ears. "I'm going to come again."

She comes, her pussy clenching, tightening around me and that's fucking it. As if by some miracle I realize I haven't put a condom on. How the fuck did I forget that?! So in the moment I didn't even think to put one on.

"Oh shit, I'm going to come," I say.

"I'm on the pill," she says through hazy eyes and I can't believe we're having this conversation right now, but a few seconds later I come rope after rope inside her. Feels so damn good. When I'm done. our bodies collapse against each other and I stay throbbing inside her. She grips me hard around my back like she doesn't want me to leave.

"You're really gripping me hard," I say.

"I like this feeling." Her sweaty body curves into me, and she grips the back of my neck.

"Me too," I admit. "But I should probably pull out now."

"You're right." she says, and I do. When she's done or when I'm done and I go grab that same work-out towel that I used the other day we clean up. We don't say much, our bodies having said more than we ever could in words.

We just sit there and sip our tequila and let the rain nail the outside windowpanes with its soft drizzles. I let her naked body collapse into mine and we fall asleep just like that.

CHAPTER 17

rett

I OPEN MY EYES, and a rush of adrenaline pounds through me.

I'm naked on Sebastian's office couch.

And I'm alone.

My heart wrenches, and I move to put on my clothes. A minute later though, before I can even locate them, the smell of fresh coffee fills the air. The door opens and Sebastian bounds in with a gigantic smirk on his face.

"Don't put your clothes on just yet," he says as he walks through the door frame. "Let's have coffee first. It's not even 5:30 a.m."

"Well first of all, I thought you'd left me and second of all, you have your clothes on. So it's not equal," I say, nodding toward him.

He's got athletic shorts, a T-Shirt, and gym shoes on. He hands me a breakfast sandwich and a cup of coffee.

"My clothing situation can quickly be rectified."

I laugh and muster a smile.

"I'll take that as a yes. Do you need anything else, Princess?" He winks.

Sebastian sets down his coffee and breakfast sandwich, slips off his shoes, and takes off his shirt.

"That will be ok for right now. But it's early," I say as I sit down on the couch. He joins me.

"But you're not afraid that someone's going to come in and see us here or see what we're doing now?" I ask as take the first sip of coffee.

"Nah," he says. "No one would dare come into the boss's office early in the morning and spy on me. Oh, wait, except for one person." He shoots a knowing glance my way.

I snigger.

"It's true that I came in and saw you, but I needed to know what was going on in here. I was hearing strange noises. I thought you might be hooking up with someone."

He laughs. We lean back in the chair enjoying our coffee and breakfast as we wake up together.

"Because hooking up in this office would be totally inappropriate."

"Well...it's okay when it's you and I. Hey, are we going to keep doing this?" I ask.

"Doing what?" He shoots the question back to me. "Do you mean just hooking up? I don't see why not."

"No, I mean every morning for the last two mornings we wrote out a fantasy and then we've done it, or we've acted out one of our fantasies. How long can we keep this up?"

Sebastian shrugs.

"I mean I have a very active and long imagination, so I can go one year, two years...

"Stop," I say, pushing him gently in the shoulder. I take a bit out of the sausage and egg breakfast sandwich.

"Why?" he asks, shooting me a somewhat suspicious glance. "Are you saying you want to stop?"

I swallow down the food. Not so shockingly, I'm famished from all of our activity last night. "No, not at all. I was just thinking about it that's all".

"Thinking about it, so you have or have not thought about today's fantasy?" I smile a little sheepishly and look down at Sebastian's feet.

"This is one that I've been thinking about for a while. I don't know if I'm ready for it to be honest."

"*You're* not ready for it? Well, we can always take a break or not do anything for a little while, go back to being just friends."

I laugh. "Yeah like that's ever going to happen now."

"What, we can always go back to being just friends."

"I don't know how I could after knowing how good you can make me feel."

He leans across and kisses me on the lips. I taste the coffee in his mouth and it's glorious. Electricity shoots through me, jolting me, making me feel awake even this early in the morning. I moan as he sticks his tongue into me. I wonder if he tastes the same coffee I do.

"You can trust me; I hope you know that by now," I muse.

"I know I can trust you but I don't know, this fantasy is really dirty," he counters.

"Dirtier than you crawling under the desk and going down on me during the fucking webcam conference meeting?"

I laugh. "Maybe, I guess it depends on your point of view."

"So are you going to tell me this one?"

"I would, but aren't we playing the whole 'write about it, don't talk about it' game?"

"I suppose so. Zane and Lacy are one lucky couple, am I right?"

"That book is going to be a freaking bestseller when you're done with it."

"Stop, it's just a silly little project. To be honest, I don't even know why I'm doing it. It's not like I'm that good of a writer or anything like that."

His smile fades. And suddenly he looks very serious almost grim. He takes hold of my chin, turns me toward him, and looks me dead in the eye.

"Hey, I don't want to hear you say things like that."

"Like what?"

"I don't want to hear you talking about you're not good enough, you are good enough. You're good enough for anything. All you have to do is decide that that's what you're doing and you'll do it, do you understand that?"

"I guess." I shrug.

He grabs hold of my thigh. "No, not you guess, you *do*. You do understand you're a fucking brilliant writer and that book you're writing is the first step on your way to becoming a bestseller. Got that, Brett?"

His dark brown eyes gaze deep into me, and I feel as though he's approaching the entrance to my soul. A warm feeling washes over me and I'm not sure what it means.

"No one has ever really believed in me. Why do you think I can actually make it?"

"Why do I believe so much in you? Let me think." He rubs his forehead with his thumb and forefinger.

"You know, it's kind of a sixth sense I've had since I've been little, but I can always tell when a person is bullshitting me or themselves. I don't know how I know, but I do know that last night, when I was looking you in the eye I was feeling you, the real you. You feel genuine Brett, you're talented and you have a spirit that uplifts others around you. Maybe you can't see it because you're you. You don't see the effect you have on people. And I swear to God it's there. And if you don't realize that yet well, I'm going to help you. You are a fucking genius. Now all you have to do is choose your path. Hell, if it's writing romances you're going to be fucking successful at it trust me. I can tell with every word I read from Zane and Lacy. I get fucking turned on."

I giggle. "You do?"

"Yeah, whenever I read your writing, I've had to relieve myself a couple of times."

"No, get out of here."

"Yes, no exaggeration."

"You're so fucking silly," I chide.

"Hey, can I ask you a question?" he retorts, his tone serious again.

"Yeah."

"Why did you agree to work here?"

"Why did I agree to work here? What kind of a question is that?"

He takes a sip of his coffee before he elaborates. This isn't the kind of conversation I expect to be having so early in the morning. But then, I haven't expected a thing that's happened between me and Sebastian.

"Yeah, I mean you're good here, don't get me wrong. But your heart is obviously in this writing thing. So why are you wasting your time at a corporate place like Blackwell Industries?"

"You know I ask myself that too sometimes." I sigh. "But in the end I thought it might provide a little bit of security. I mean, after I bounced from job to job, and I guess I just wanted to try something new. When you reached out to me I was flattered that you would even consider me for a company like this without having a college degree."

"So you're insecure that you don't have a college degree?"

"Yes." I nod. I take a sip of my coffee and enjoy the warm feeling on my throat. The sun is starting to rise higher on the horizon, and a reddish-orange glow starts to show through the office window.

"I think a college degree is worth less and less. It's more of a fancy pile of paper that comes with a bunch of student loans. It doesn't mean you're smarter or dumber than anyone else. I personally didn't go to college, so maybe I'm biased, but I'm glad I didn't, even though some days people look at me and I can tell that's what they think of me. That look in their eyes says it all. They think Sebastian Blackwell is just a lucky son of a bitch who won the lottery. They have no idea about how hard I've worked to make this happen. They don't know what it's like losing your first million then going all-in on an investment with your last pennies, only to have that one come through. I'm ranting now, but all I'm saying is you're smart as fuck, Brett. I know that."

My chest swells with pride at hearing Sebastian say those words. He's so sincere, I can tell he truly means them.

"Thank you. I guess I'm smart. I'll accept your compliment."

Breaching the space between us, he uses his finger to tip my chin into him and he kisses me on the lips. I feel his sexy stubble on my cheek.

"So changing topics," I continue. "I do have a conundrum I'm in right now, I can't wear the same clothes I wore yesterday in the office, people will think it's weird if they notice. They'll think I'm homeless or something."

"Tell me your size," Sebastian says without hesitation. "I will have some clothes brought in."

"But won't people suspect that when they see me wearing them that I'm yours? Like your assistant could tell people. And this is a small town."

He takes a deep breath, and rakes a hand through his hair. "You're right and fuck, I love hearing you say that, but you don't want to be seen with me, right?"

"Oh well." I hesitate. It's not that I don't want to be seen with him but I also really don't want the other employees to think that I'm receiving any type of special treatment from the boss. "You know what", I say. "I'll text my friend Crystal. She probably hasn't left yet and we're the same size, so I'll have her bring something. She won't ask questions, she's a good friend."

"Whatever you want."

"But I should get moving," I say. "The early risers will probably start getting to the office soon, right?"

"Stay a few more minutes. Come on," he chides.

I slide my hand on his thigh and feel between his legs. He lets out a low moan and I respond by moaning a little bit as well. "I really need to go."

"Yeah you fucking do, oh gosh you fucking do," he mutters. "So don't do that, don't get me all worked up if you're just going to leave."

"Alright, I'm getting up. No more teasing." I jump to my feet, finally, and Sebastian looks slightly disappointed.

"Go on, get out of here, Miss Blue. I'll get you back for this." He winks.

I text Crystal then change into the clothes I wore yesterday. I kiss Sebastian goodbye for the morning. Luckily, I catch Crystal right before she's leaving her house. A half hour later she meets me in the local coffee shop *Grinds* for the handoff.

"Hey. Good morning!" she says cheerily. She walks up to me at the table I'm sitting at, sipping my coffee and reading the local newspaper since my phone is close to dying.

"Hey yourself," I say as she hands me the bag.

"I got something cool, something I thought you'd like. A blue dress."

"Oh that's perfect," I say. "Thanks so much."

"So..." Crystal says, letting her voice trail off and taking a seat across from me.

"So what?" I imitate; as if I don't know what she's about to say.

"Oh come on," she says. "You really aren't going to give me any more information?"

I take a deep breath. If I tell her I signed an NDA. is that breaking the code? "It's complicated," I say.

"Oh stop it. I told you about the time when I gave Bobby McCallum a hand job underneath the bleachers in twelfth grade. Honestly, that was a low point. I'm not saying you're having a little boy right now, I'm just saying I'm curious so, no information for your best bud?

I take a deep breath. "I can tell you that it's no one you know personally, and I just had a good fun night," I admit, giving her little detail to work with.

She laughs. "Going to keep things vague, well all right, I see how it is."

I want to make sure she knows that I don't mean to keep things from her. "Look, I will tell you about it the instant it's important, but right now it's just not that big of a deal. Yet."

I wonder if Sebastian and I could ever be a *thing*, but I have my doubts.

"Fine," she retorts, though I can tell she was excited for some juicy gossip.

"But let me buy you some coffee to return the favor." I get her drink, a grande vanilla sweet cream iced coffee, and hand it over to her.

"So how is your book going?" she asks.

"My book?"

"Uh yeah. The romance novel you were telling me about. That was like when you started this job, right? I'm just thinking you're making progress so I'm curious how it's going."

"Oh that thing, it's going ok. You know. Chipping away at it."

"Like, have you been getting any inspiration or...oh. I know," she says, tapping her nose. "This one-night stand guy is your inspiration! Aha! It all makes sense now."

"I don't like writing about one-night stands anyways."

"I'm just throwing out possibilities. You're saying you don't get *any* inspiration from him?"

"The book is going pretty well," I say, trying to skirt the subject. I'm sure I'm probably blushing. "I can let you read it in a little bit, I'm almost done with it, about two-thirds of the way through."

"I can't wait to read it," she says, taking a big suck of her iced coffee.

"I can't wait to be done with it."

"By the way, my little sister is really getting good at designing covers so if you need anyone..."

"I'm pretty sure your little sister is too young for this kind of book," I cut her off.

"Oh shoot, well she can still make the cover, right?"

"I suppose there's no harm in that."

"Have you thought of a title for the book yet?"

"I haven't actually. I have no idea what I'm gonna call it."

"Ok well, I have some ideas when you're ready." She takes a sip of her coffee and looks me in the eye.

"You've been thinking about this a lot, haven't you?" I giggle.

"Yeah actually. I was thinking about it the whole ride over here so I'm kind of an expert now at titles."

"Alright. What do you think it should be called?"

"Well, I was thinking it's about a boss right and it's got a lot of hot scenes in it, so how about 'The Boss's Office Slut'?"

I laugh. "I'd like to think that she's a little bit more than a slut."

"Hmm, okay. Well, maybe she's not a slut slut, but she's slut-*y*, like in an empowering way. Oh! What about the 'Boss's Innocent Slut Virgin'?"

I chuckle. "That just sounds like a bunch of buzzwords struck together."

"It sounded better in my head," she says. "Anyways, what were you thinking for the title?"

"I was thinking something more like; well they have a benefit situation so, 'Boss Man with Benefits.'"

"'Boss Man with Benefits,'" she says out loud. "That's actually not bad. You came up with that all on your own?"

"Yeah."

"I like that." She looks at her watch and sighs. "Anyway, I need to get to work. Speaking of boss, my boss has been working my ass off lately and not in a good way. Although he's a little bit too old for me."

"Hey, maybe you got some inspiration there for me," I say. She chuckles as we both walk out the door together. She turns to leave but before she does, she asks me a question that makes me think.

"So just friends with benefits? Is that like the kind of situation you have set up with your man toy or whatever you're getting these clothes for? Your one-night stand you had last night? Or is the title just pure fiction."

I sigh. "Honestly--I'm not sure. It's not really a benefits situation. At least I'd like to think it's more than that."

"Well, you know how guys think. He's probably fine with the situation as it is. Anyways I got to run, catch you later, boo."

She heads off and I'm left with a thought; is that all Sebastian Blackwell wants with me? He seems quite fine just to keep things casual. I take a breath. I don't have time to think about this. It's too much right now, I have another fantasy to write.

I need to get this book done with, and with one third of it to go, I'm nearly in the homestretch of my novel.

THAT MORNING AT WORK, I type up a fantasy that I want to do today with Sebastian.

Screw it. This isn't even about Lacy and Zane any more. I might as well stop kidding myself.

This morning's scene is very over the top, and I'm a little worked up when I'm done with it.

It's so filthy I can't even believe that I'm the one who's writing this.

But this is what Sebastian does to me. He brings out the dirty in me.

I do wonder if he'll think I'm just really dirty, or if he'll think differently of me now that he knows I'm capable of being this dirty.

I try not to overthink it. But this one is even worse than the under the table fantasy.

I hit send in my email that includes the text of the next chapter between Zane and Lacy. Five minutes later, a message pops up on my screen from Mr. X.

Mr. X: Are you fucking serious with this?? Lacy is a very very dirty girl in this chapter

I clam up, I'm a little bit nervous now even more so than when I typed it.

BRETT: What, you don't think you can handle it?

Mr. X: Oh I can handle it. The question is can you handle the spin on this. Lacy wants to be taken like that in the office. The how she wants to have a quickie is clear. But I might play with the where.

Brett: I handled your little under the table strategy, so I think I'll be ok with whatever you have in store for me with this

Mr. X: Do you even know me? It's like we haven't been sleeping together for one night

Brett: Ha. Good one.

Mr. X: I can't wait for this one. You are such an incredible writer. And I love your filthy mind.

Brett: Is it weird that when you say you love my mind that turns me on?

Mr. X: It is weird. You're fucking weird. I'm weird too. Couple of weirdos who are going to do some weird stuff later

Brett: I love that you're accepting of my weirdo-ness

Mr X: It's my favorite part about you. Btw make sure you have a light lunch today. I don't want you to get too... shall we say, sleepy

Brett: How can I get sleepy when I have a boss as sexy as you?

Mr. X: Good point, plus I'm the most interesting one that does presenting in this building. I'll see you at 1:30 for the meeting. Don't be late.

Even though he's not near me, I can picture him winking with that mischievous 'I know something you don't' look in his eye, and my heart skips a beat. I wonder what he's got in store for me.

CHAPTER 18

ebastian

AFTER I READ what Brett writes me today, it's all I can do not to walk around with a hard-on at the office. I know this romance novel that she's writing is just that; a novel. It's fiction, it's made up, it's not real. Yet when I read about Lacy and Zane I just wonder what she thought about last night. She said she doesn't want to be serious, but maybe there is a chance. Fuck, I think, leaning back in my office chair. I'm so hard I want to get after it right now.

Over the years, yeah sure, I've rubbed a few out in my office, I'm not going to lie. But usually I wasn't thinking about anyone specific. Now, I'm thinking specifically about a girl I barely know and goddamn it, I might even be falling for her; fuck. It makes no sense, it all happened so quickly. I shake my head out and tighten my tie. I need to stay focused; it's only 10:00 am, and I still have a lot of work to do with that distillery project before I can think about taking a break.

I look through the designs of the new two-story factory that we're building. The project will employ over 500 people from Blackwell. It will bring in a whole hunk of tax revenue for the area and last but not least, the people of the town are going to have access to what they need most in this world; fresh whisky. Yeah, sure I'll make a little money here too but it feels better thinking of the project as a sort of goodwill; that I'm making it possible for all the people the world to get their drink on.

Finally, I'm able to get into the work I have to do. I grab lunch then prep for the 1:30 meeting that I'm going to be running. When I go into the meeting room, everyone is standing around. I motion for them to get into the circular desk and we get to work. Halfway through the meeting, I clasp my hands together and ask if anyone has any questions; they don't, so fantastic.

"All right then, if you don't have any questions, I assume you all know your roles here, so let's dismiss early."

They seem eager about the early dismissal and head out of the room and into the elevator. I pick my path of attack; carefully walking right behind Brett. She looks fucking lovely today. I watch her ass as it wiggles in the blue dress that she got from her friend. We stand nonchalantly waiting for the elevator. The shiny silver doors finally flash open and we get in. Me, Troy, and Brett are headed up.

"Hey Brett," Troy says, standing right in front of me. "I was just wanting to ask you something."

"Ask away," she says. She switches her hair over the side of her ear, a little bit surprised.

"Yeah, I wanted to ask; are you going to go to the happy hour later?"

Jealousy rises in my stomach as I watch the two interact. As much as I want to get mad at Troy, I can't hate on him for what he's doing. Who the hell wouldn't want to go to the happy hour with Brett? She's the fucking prize of the office as far as I'm concerned. I watch the interaction curiously; Brett in front of me, to my left, and Troy in front of me to my right. He's definitely checking her out. I think my angle is better though.

"I would love to go to happy hour," Brett smiles, "but I've just been putting in some really long hours at work and I was planning on catching up on some rest later. I'm sorry, I'm going to have to take a rain check."

"That's all right," Troy says. And I can tell he's trying genuinely not to sound surprised or dejected; even though he is. "It's not a big deal at all, just thought I'd ask, maybe some other time."

"Yes, sure," she agrees. "maybe some other time." Troy nods as the elevator comes to a stop at floor fourteen.

"All right well, guess I'll see you cats at the next meeting," he says as he steps out.

He disappears down the hallway, and the elevator dings shut.

Then it's just Brett and I together in the elevator alone. Brett exhales.

"I'm so slammed today. So much work to do this afternoon."

"Yeah, you are slammed," I say with a smirk. I press the emergency stop button on the elevator and it comes to a halt. Brett freezes.

"Oh my gosh, what on Earth are you doing"?

"Well, according to Lacy and Zane, Lacy wanted to get caught off guard today."

"Here?" she gasps.

"Yes," I confirm, smirking. "Right fucking here."

I pin her body hard up against the clean silver metal of

the elevator. She moans beneath me as I take hold of her hot creamy thighs, dragging my hand up the back of them. I grab her ass.

"But we're not *actually* going to do it here, are we? There's a camera. Isn't someone going to see, the security guard maybe?" She nods toward the digital surveillance camera that's been placed in the elevator.

"So," I grunt. "What do you care if we give them a little show?"

She laughs. "Aren't we supposed to be keeping this a secret?" I look at her sky blue eyes dead on.

"Don't worry. I did a little project this morning. As in, I replaced that camera with a personal camera."

She raises an eyebrow. "So this will be saved for what exactly?"

I shrug. "I mean, I figured I could give you a copy to watch after we're done and that way you could take notes, just in case you wanted to go back and add some of this in and see what happens between Lacy and Zane."

"Oh so thoughtful of you, Bossman." I let my hands drift up her stomach and sneak them underneath her bra. She moans so I grab both of her tits. I search for and find her nipples, delicately running my thumbs across them. They're hard, standing on end.

"If you don't want to do this we don't have to." I smirk.

"Stop teasing me. Just fuck me," she begs in a whisper. "Please."

Her voice is low, as if she's embarrassed she wants it this bad. I tip her chin to me. "Brett, you're so damn sexy. I couldn't stop thinking the whole meeting how I was going to do this with you."

She hesitates, and I take the time to cover her mouth with mine for a kiss. Our bodies gyrate against each other as we make out in the elevator.

I love the feeling of her hips spurring against me, and I reciprocate her sense of urgency. There will be a time for hour long lovemaking sessions between us in the future, but right now, this is about giving Brett what she wanted; what she wrote about:

A dirty quickie that takes her by surprise.

My cock is so hard now, I could cut diamonds with it. She runs her hand over my pants and gets busy undoing my belt, taking down my zipper. In the confined space, the entire elevator fills with her perfumed scent mixed with our sweat. Her breath smells like cherry lip gloss and freshness and sex and everything that's good in the world. I wrap my arms around her body, feeling every inch of her flesh available to me within my reach. I want to feel her in every way possible. I run my hand under her clothes over her back, bring them around to her stomach, and gently up to her breasts. She reaches inside my pants, grabs hold of my cock, and whispers in my ear; her voice soft and throaty. "Bossman, I want you so bad right now."

"And what Brett wants, Brett gets," I murmur. I reach between her legs, she's already soaking wet. I flick her clit for a few moments with my finger, letting her soft moans spur on my enthusiasm. I love the way she sounds when she's turned on like this. She anxiously pulls down my pants and briefs with one motion, and my cock flops out. Her jaw drops.

She drops to her knees and takes me into her mouth, sucking the tip. I lean back and groan. Fuck, she feels amazing. I look down and watch her blonde hair bobbing back and forth.

I can't believe how dirty innocent little Brett is capable of being with me.

And I love it.

I don't think H.R. would be okay with this if they knew it

was going on. But then again, I can't think very clearly right now with my cock inches deep in Brett's mouth. She takes me whole, sending pleasure rocking from my spine through my entire body.

"Fuck, Brett," I moan. "What are you doing to me?" She glances up at me and doesn't say a thing, she just smiles as she runs her hand back and forth on the shaft of my cock. I smile down at her and take a mental snapshot for posterity. This is one of those moments in life you can't get back, one of those moments that you don't have a camera with you to take that picture. But I'll definitely remember this one forever. Brett's ruby red lips locked around my cock as we lock eyes. I grip and massage her neck and lean down.

"Baby, stand up," I growl into her ear.

She does as she's told, and stands before me. I reach under her dress, pull down her panties, and pull her into me, nibbling at her ear and growling.

"Turn your gorgeous body around, Princess."

Without a word, she turns around and sticks her arms out to brace herself for what she knows is coming. Well, she'll be coming too but first, I hike her blue dress up above her ass and look down at the luscious round thing.

"Holy fucking shit, baby. I'm so hard right now. It's fucking awesome. Are you ready for this?" She groans.

"Just fuck me already will you. Please."

I push in just the tip. She's tight and still swollen from last night. I gently push in a few inches and start to move a little bit.

"Relax baby."

"It's big though."

"And you're so tight." I chuckle.

"Maybe it's a little bit of both," she says. Gradually, I thrust in deeper. Pleasure runs through my spine; through my whole body. Just touching her makes me electric. I grab onto her hips and thrust all the way in; she lets out a stifled moan when I bottom out.

CHAPTER 19

rett

THE NEXT COUPLE of weeks at Blackwell Industries are very intense. And when I say intense, I'm referring to a variety of areas.

To start with, Sebastian and I do it in almost every room in the Blackwell Building we can reasonably hook up in.

The janitor closet.

The gym.

His secretary's desk when we're doing a little role-playing.

The list goes on and on.

But there's more. I finish with Lacy and Zane's story, so now I'm in the editing phase of the book.

Meanwhile, I'm trying to keep everything afloat that I'm doing for my day job.

Somehow, Sebastian and I haven't been found out yet. The way we're sneaking around, it only feels like a matter of time until we slip up, or a weird coincidence results in us getting caught.

My responsibilities at this job have shifted, too. Sebastian claims he has nothing to do with my added responsibility, and that it's been mostly Bob's idea.

But today, I'm tasked with reaching out to distributors to help find a way for the distillery to open its doors two months early.

As I sit at my desk, what I really want to be doing is editing my novel. It's almost to the point where I'm confident enough to let Crystal read it. She's been bugging me to show her the book for a while.

I click off the browser I'm using for work stuff and click back onto the Google document where I have the first draft of my book saved.

As I skim the book, a fear pops into my head: If Crystal reads the book, and she knows that I have a real life inspiration for the book, won't she immediately realize that I've been sleeping with Sebastian Blackwell all this time?

I run a hand through my hair and lean back in my chair, taking a deep breath. I don't like thinking about Crystal--or anyone--knowing what I've been up to at my new job.

My paranoia has nothing to do with the NDA I signed either.

My problem has more to do with my own negative self-judgment.

I've felt more sexually liberated with Sebastian than I ever thought was possible.

Yet another part of me though, feels off with how things are between us.

I don't want to be *that girl*, asking about where the relationship is going when Sebastian has a million important things on his mind every day.

But I can't help but think, is this it?

Is this as far as we'll get with the emotional profundity of our relationship? I'm grateful for the inspiration he's given me. But will we ever be something more?

Then again, I didn't come into this looking for a marriage proposal.

I scroll through the exploits of Lacy and Zane, noting where they did it in the different chapters. Their love life is more or less a mirror of the sex life between Sebastian and I, except theirs has a happy ending. Sebastian has even written a healthy amount of the chapters from Zane's point of view.

When I started this job and this benefits situation with my boss I figured it wouldn't last very long. Maybe it would be a one-night thing. But now, the way I'm thinking about him, everything has changed.

I decide I need to tell him how I feel.

"Brett," a voice says over my shoulder. "What are you working on, honey?"

My heart lurches when I realize two things. One, this is Bob looking over my shoulder, and I absolutely don't want him to see the dirty words on the screen, and start asking questions about what I'm doing during work hours. Two, Bob just called me *honey*.

"Oh, nothing," I say in a sing-song voice, minimizing the Google Docs browser.

"Really?" he says, crossing his arms. "Because that sure as hell didn't look like nothing. I think I saw some dirty words on the screen. What exactly are you writing? I hope it wouldn't be anything to violate the rules of the handbook."

Before I can stop him, Bob leans in and moves the mouse to bring back up the Google document that houses my erotic novel. I freeze like a deer in headlights.

As Bob scrolls, the novel happens to be on a particularly dirty session between Zane and Lacy.

In an elevator. I wonder where I got that inspiration.

"What the...what the hell?! Oh my gosh, is this a sex scene? About a boss and employee?"

For a moment Bob looks at me like I'm a sexual object for his taking, which sends a cold shiver down my spine. I want to tell him so badly that I'm taken, and I want to tell him by who.

But I can't.

"You know, that's weird...I think my friend sent me that Google document," I say, nudging Bob's hand, taking the mouse, and exiting out of the document. "She was playing a trick on me I think."

I muster a partial smile.

Bob's face turns part sinister, part creepy. "You know. If you ever need anything Brett, I'm here for you."

"I'm good, thanks. Anyways I have a lot of work to do so I'm going to get to it."

Bob leans back, his hands on his hips. He furrows his brow.

"You know what? I don't like your snarky attitude."

"Snarky? I'm not snarky at all!"

"There. See that snark! Denying it again. I think I'm going to put you on notice with HR."

My heart races a little bit, and I'm not sure why Bob is being such a dick all of a sudden. "Human Resources?"

"That's right. I don't know what they'd think of you typing such a weird thing at work. Or even pulling it up on your computer, for that matter."

The last thing I want is a complaint lodged with Human Resources, and for them to start digging deeper into everything. God only knows what the consequences would be if they have access to all of my files.

As if things can't get any worse, Kim Murphy must have heard the commotion between us, and out of the corner of my eye I see her approaching.

"Hello." She smiles callously. "What's all the commotion about?"

Bob sneers. "It seems like Brett here has a habit of getting off task. She won't tell me exactly what she's working on, but it's making me suspicious.

As if he's got a radar that senses everything, Sebastian suddenly materializes behind Bob.

"Everything all right here?" his voice booms, and Bob launches into the explanation again.

"No." Bob crosses his arms. "As a matter of fact, everything's not alright. Your new hire here is working on some rather illicit materials during work hours."

Sebastian rocks back on his heel and crosses his arms as if he's very upset. "You don't say. What's this all about, Brett? Is this true?"

I swallow. "I told Bob. It was just a note that a friend sent me. I shouldn't have opened it at work. It was a mistake. I won't do it again."

"I'm going to let Human resources know. I don't trust her, to be honest, Sir," Bob says. "Her productivity numbers are quite low for a girl who spends so much time here. I have a feeling she's been working on something non-work related."

Sebastian rubs a hand and finger on his chin, as if he is thinking hard. "No," he says. "Don't call HR. You know what, let me handle this one personally. Brett, come on into my office."

"Are you sure?" Kim interrupts. "You have so much on your plate lately. I feel like you've been missing some meetings and people don't know where you are."

A guilty feeling wooshes through me, because for many of those missed meetings, I'm the one he was with. I absolutely do not want to go with Kim, though.

Sebastian squints, mulling it over.

"I'll handle it. Come with me, Brett."

His voice is dominant-sounding, and a little different than the tone he usually uses with me.

It's his boss voice.

"Yes Sir," I say. I get up, lock my computer, and follow behind Sebastian, feeling the disapproving gaze of Bob at my back.

Kim scowls even harder at me, and I feel a tinge of jealousy coming from her for the added attention Sebastian is giving me.

Or maybe I'm just imagining that. I can't tell.

When we arrive at his office, Fiona greets me with a smile. "Oh hi, Brett," she says and stands up. "I didn't know you had a ten a.m. appointment today. Is this on the schedule?"

"Not on the schedule," Sebastian booms. "Clear my morning. I have something I need to deal with."

"Oh," she says, glancing at me. "Will do."

Sebastian opens the door to his office. "After you, Miss Blue."

"Thank you."

I walk into Sebastian's office, and just knowing I'm in his lair, in his space, turns me on. I've been with him so often in here lately, my body already revs up just by stepping inside his office and being near his presence.

I sit down in the chair, cross my legs, and straighten out the black skirt I have on today.

Sebastian grabs a glass of water and leans against his desk. His light blue suit glimmers in the morning sunlight seeping through the window.

"How are you doing? Bob fuck with you?"

"Bob is acting really weird," I say. "And he saw me pull up the document with Lacy and Zane's story. I'm worried he's going to report me to HR and they'll start looking into my computer usage. You know, like you did."

Sebastian nods and takes a sip of his water, his gaze steely. "That could be an issue."

"Is that something they might do?" I ask.

The thought crosses my mind that I don't want to be talking about the logistics of getting caught.

I really just wish we were out in the open. Sneaking around has been fun, but it's getting old.

"They certainly have the power to do so. But I also have the power to tell them to look the other way. Rex is the head of HR. He's a good friend. I've hired him personally. I'll make sure he squashes any reports coming in."

I rub my forehead with two fingers. "Sebastian, can I ask you a question?"

"Uh oh. One of those questions that has to be prefaced by you asking me a question."

"What, are you nervous?"

"I have ice in my veins," he says with a smirk. "There's not much that makes me nervous anymore. What's your question?"

I get up from my chair and walk over to him. He watches me closely. I swear he doesn't even blink.

"Fuck, you look sexy today," he says with a wide grin.

"We're not changing the subject," I say. "I want to know something. You'll think it's silly though."

"It's not silly if you're thinking it. What is it?"

I sigh, and put my hand on his forearm. His body feels hot. "It's just that, what are we *doing* here, you and me?"

Sebastian rakes a hand through his hair. "What are we...*doing?*" he snorts. "I mean I think we've been having a great time getting to know each other. That's what we've been doing."

I bite my lip. "I don't disagree with you on that. But I've been thinking. Is that all we are? Just great sex? Is that all I am to you?"

"Is that all *I* am to *you*? Look Brett, you were the one who started using me for inspiration for your romance novel. And you're going to say...I mean what are you asking exactly? I don't understand. I thought this was the way you wanted it."

I take a step closer to him and he wraps his arms around me. "You need me to spell it out for you?"

"Yes." He lowers his hands down my back, and cups my ass through my skirt. I moan a little. I hate that he has such control over me and my pleasure.

"Okay. Well, you've said some really nice things about me in the past few weeks. You've said how it 'doesn't make any sense' that I exist. But I do exist. And I'm here. And I want you. I like you."

"Brett. I don't know what you want from me. You stated what you wanted going into this--a boss with benefits. Someone to play out your sexual fantasies with. I've been that person, and I've had a great time with you."

I look into Sebastian's gorgeous brown eyes. I notice for the first time he's got flits of blue around his irises, too. "How have I not noticed your eyes have a little bit of blue in them," I blurt out, squinting.

His expression turns quizzical. "What are you talking about?"

"I notice something new about you every day." I smile. "I want to keep noticing things about you."

"Why are you being so veiled right now? You know I don't understand womanspeak," he says as he pulls my body into his. I love the way his muscular chest feels pressed up against me when he holds me tight.

I push him away. "I like you, Sebastian! A lot. Of course I like the sex. You're a freaking sex god. But I want more. I need more, if this is going to work out."

He pauses and arches an eyebrow. "Work out...like long-term? What do you mean?"

I exhale. I don't know if he's deliberately not understanding me, or if real romance beyond hooking up is the one area where Sebastian turns dumb.

"I need a drink," I say, and head to the bar in Sebastian's office. I pour myself a ten a.m. tequila, and I feel like I'm in the show Mad Men, where they drink at all hours of the day.

"I'll join you," he says. "Pour one for me."

I pour another and hand it to him. He joins me on the couch, sinking in and putting his arm up along the lip of the sofa.

"Look, I get it," he says. "What you're feeling, I've been feeling it too. We need to have this talk at some point. So let's have it. You're special to me, Brett. This whole thing between us, I know you've said you've learned a lot. So have I. I mean we've lived out so many of your sexual fantasies. Mine too. I feel comfortable with you in a way I've never felt with anyone. It's like the world is our oyster. I'm not sure why I feel so comfortable with you, but I do."

He fists a bunch of my hair, and my breath hitches. "I feel like I could tell you just about anything too, and you wouldn't judge me for it."

His brow furrows and he squeezes my shoulder lightly. "Is there...something you haven't told me yet?"

I shrug, thinking about a certain fantasy that's been cropping up in my subconscious lately. I don't know where it comes from, but it's been nipping at me late at night when I toss and turn in my bed. Now that Sebastian's opened Pandora's Box for me, I can't deny it's something I want.

Instead of telling him straight up though, I ask Sebastian a question.

"Do you have any hard limits?"

"Hard limits. Let me think. I wouldn't do a dirty sanchez, Cleveland steamer, or probably not the angry pirate—I don't like those weird ones."

I roll my eyes. "I'm being serious, Sebastian. I'm going to tell you something but you can't judge me, okay? What's a Cleveland Steamer anyway?"

"It's where I take a dump on your chest and then titty fuck you," he says with a straight face.

"I think I'm going to throw up," I say. "Does anyone actually *do* that?"

He shrugs. "Lot of interesting people out there. Personally not my cup of tea but, hey, who am I to judge."

I shiver. "That's gross."

"So that's not what you've been dreaming about? Okay, I think I can get on board with whatever you want then. I'm curious as to why you're hesitant to tell me. You know you can tell me anything."

I swallow, and exhale slowly.

"I want to have a threesome."

The words hang in the air, and second pass.

Sebastian's jaw drops in shock. "Holy shit. Like two girls and a guy?"

"No, like one girl and two guys."

My face turns bright red as I watch Sebastian process this information.

Sebastian takes a long slow pull on his drink. "As much as I would love to give you everything you want, I think seeing you with another guy is a hard limit for me."

"Okay. It's alright. Forget I brought it up. I'm sorry."

He narrows his gaze at me. "But this is something you've thought about. Something you really want."

I nod. "I think so. But maybe this is where the buck stops. Maybe this is one fantasy that's truly meant to stay as just that--a fantasy. Maybe this one isn't meant to be."

"I want to give you everything," Sebastian says, his voice more hoarse than usual. "Let me think about it. And let's cool it for now with these daytime meetings."

"Are you saying you're done being my inspiration for Zane? Most of the book is done, but just in case I want to--" I choose my word carefully, "--revise any scenes with you."

He chuckles. "I'm saying we should lay low while Human Resources is on the lookout for us. Besides, I want to do something different this week."

He reaches in his pocket and hands me a key. "Take a break for this week. We've got a lot of work to do on the distillery project and the ranch, so this will be a good time to put our heads down and get work done. Plus, I'm traveling for a few days this week. But now you've got the keys to my house. Wait for me on Friday evening there. No more email now. Just texting. Sound good?"

I nod as I take the key. My heart warms that he's trusting me to be alone in his house. "So you want me to be your little present all wrapped up for you when you get home?"

He puts his finger on my chin and tips me toward him.

"Exactly. Think you can do that?"

"I think I definitely can." I swallow down the rest of my tequila and plant a firm kiss on his lips. "Now I better get back to the floor. Like you said, we don't want to be suspicious anymore this week. That starts now."

I walk out of the office, and the vibe feels a little different from what we've been so far. I can't help but think something big is about to happen between us. I'm glad the threesome thing seemed to have been brushed off. Maybe he'll just forget about it, because I'm embarrassed a little bit, to tell the truth.

My mind starts to churn with ideas for how I can best greet him on Friday.

This may be our hottest encounter yet.

CHAPTER 20

ebastian

THE END of the week can't come soon enough. After our close call with Bob wanting to report Brett to Human Resources, I decide I need to think over some things.

Our relationship, at least on a sexual level, has been rocketing along.

As my limo driver takes me back to my place where she'll be waiting for me, I look out the window at Blackwell and think about what we could become.

I need to tell her how I really feel. I've been going back and forth back and forth thinking about if she's worthy of the L word. It's a word that I've never told anyone in seriousness.

I was close to telling one girl, years ago, in my early 20s but that never panned out. So now it's just something that I need to tell her.

Truthfully though, I've been in love with Brett since the first time.

She needs to know that in spite of the casualness of this relationship, things have been progressing in a way that--dammit--I could see myself being with her long-term. And I need to know if she feels the same way. Since the beginning, she's made it very clear what I am to her. I'm her hook up buddy and sure I'm also her boss. She's using me as fodder for her book.

And I have a feeling it's going to be a bestseller. She writes with the same hot fire she fucks with. Which is why I need her in my life.

She's so vibrant and bubbly and happy. Not to mention kind, sexy, and beautiful. What more can a man want in a woman?

My limo driver plays a song as if right on cue. "When a Man Loves a Woman." I have to laugh a little bit. I roll down the divider window.

"Hey Barney, quite a song you got going on there." I chuckle.

"Oh sorry about that boss," he quips. "I'll turn it down."

"No, actually I was wondering if you could turn it up." I smile.

He shrugs and cranks it up as we arrive at my house. My place is an old colonial style build on the corner of Webster and Main. It's white with black trim around the windows. My great-grandfather used to own the house before his son sold it when he came on hard times. When I had the money, I bought it from the owner. It's not gated, and it's not a typical billionaire's house, but it's what I like.

The family history of the place adds a little something special for me. I smile, and I realize why I respected Brett so much when she put her foot down and refused to accept any amount of money for her family's house.

Some things are just not worth selling.

I like my house even more right now, given that Brett is inside right now, waiting for me.

"Thanks Barney," I say. "Have a good night."

"You're not going anywhere else tonight boss?" he asks.

"No," I chuckle. "I think I'll have quite enough on my plate tonight. You've got the rest of the night off."

I shut the door, and take a big inhale of fresh air. The sunset ebbs on the horizon, and I can feel the love coursing through me. This is the start of a brand new chapter in my life.

The four words are practically on my lips.

"I love you Brett," I mouth, whispering the words as I turn the key in the door.

Before I can even turn the knob, it opens, and the most beautiful girl in the world greets me.

"Hi handsome." Brett smiles up at me, and gives me a kiss on the cheek. My eyes widen when I look down at her and take a closer look at what she's wearing.

Also at what she's *not* wearing.

"Are you only wearing an apron?"

She looks up at me with a little snide glance.

"Well I was making dinner and I didn't want to get my work clothes dirty."

I sniff. The air smells positively magnificent. "Are you...baking?"

"What you smell is probably the banana bread," she says. "But I cooked you some steak and mashed potatoes. It's not much, but I figured you would be hungry after your long flight."

"Well you figured right. I am damn hungry." I grab her hips and lean into her body, kissing her against the wall. I slide my hand down the creamy flesh of her luscious ass. "How the fuck did you know this is my ultimate fantasy?"

She arches an eyebrow my way. "Lucky guess." She shrugs with a smile. "I've always wanted to answer the door like this. And I've been missing you so much this week after we decided to play it cool at the office."

My cock hardens to a steel rod as we grind against each other, making out. The door isn't even shut yet.

Brett runs her hand on the outside of my pants tracing the outline of my cock.

"Fuck baby, you've got me so hard," I groan.

"I know," she snorts, like she's the snarkiest housewife ever.

"I'm going to have to punish you for that remark," I smirk.

"Oh really? Well can I do something first?" She grins, and she's got a devilish look in her eyes. With her innocent blues looking up at me, I feel she's about to do something very naughty.

"You ready for dinner?" she asks instead, and somehow slips out from my pinning her against the wall and heads to the kitchen.

She seems to have made herself right at home here already. And I like it.

"I have to take the bread out of the oven," she says, and I follow her into my kitchen.

I watch her bend over to get the banana bread out and set it on top of the oven, and I fucking lose it.

I grab her from behind, and lift her up and onto the marble island countertop.

"What's going on?" she breathes.

"I'm having an early dinner, that's what."

I pull her apron up, spread her legs, and dive between them, licking her clit like I'm starving and she's the last meal on Earth.

She lets go; grinding into me and fucking my face as my tongue swirls around her opening.

"Oh God, this is so much better when I can watch you," she moans, grabbing onto my hair.

I pull up for a moment and let my finger linger on her clit. "Is that right? You like fucking my face, do you?"

"Yes," she moans. "I do."

"You like fucking your billionaire boss's face. Well--good news. He likes it too."

I smile and dive back between her legs, letting loose. As hot as all of our hooking up at the office has been, there's something about hooking up in the privacy of my house that is liberating.

Although, that damn door is still open. I wonder if the neighbors can hear her scream?

But I don't really give a fuck what the neighbors think anymore. I love Brett Blue, I love eating her out, and I'd do fucking anything for this girl. Just like she would apparently do for me.

I'm not sure what smells more delicious, the banana bread or her.

I wrap my hands around her ass and thighs and pull her mound into me. She leans back on the marble of the island countertop.

She quivers and shakes, and she comes.

All over my fucking face.

"Holy dear God in heaven," she mutters, and I don't know if she's saying a prayer or what.

Still shaking, she pushes my head up and off of her pussy.

"Had enough?" I wink.

She hops down from the island, her face flushed red.

"Shut up." She grins. "You and your dirty mouth are going to get me into trouble."

"How so?"

She kneels down on the floor, unzips my pants, and flops my cock out.

I groan. "I don't know what this has to do with getting in trouble, but keep doing what you're doing," I say.

She starts by licking the shaft of my cock, running her tongue from base to tip, back and forth over and over again. I put my hands on my waist.

"Hang on," I say. I take a minute to take off my shoes, socks, pants, and everything else that I'm wearing. I want this experience to be just me, her mouth, and that sexy little apron that barely covers her tits. She rubs my cock, now wet with her saliva, running her hand back and forth on my head and shaft cupping my balls as she does it.

"You are so fucking hot right now. You have no clue," I mutter as she takes me deep into her mouth, tonguing the bottom of my cock as she slides her mouth back and forth. "Do you?" I smirk.

"Ah-ah," she says, trying to shake her head but it's hard when she's got her mouth full.

She bobs back and forth on my hard length and I run my hand through her hair. She's so good, I can't help but gyrate my hips in rhythm with her bobbing head, and she takes me deep with each suck.

A few minutes later I'm fucking her face with vigor and she's gripping my ass with her hands as she sends me to pleasure island.

As badly as I want to come right now, I need to be inside her even more.

Gripping her by the hair, I gently pull her up from her knees. She's breathing hard.

I spin her around. She puts her hands out to grip the marble island, and I slide my cock into her from behind.

She's so wet from before, and I'm still slick with her saliva, so I slide right in with ease despite how tight she is.

"Mmm, Sebastian," she moans, and lays her head on the

countertop, her beautiful blonde hair spread out to the side on the table. "Fuck me."

"God damn I fucking love you," I mutter to myself, and then realize I haven't told her yet.

"You what?" she croaks, and her voice fades a little at the end of her sentence as I fuck her harder.

"I said I love...fucking you," I say, skirting the issue.

"Oh. Me too."

I thrust into her, my hips slamming into her ass, my cock reaching deeper with every stroke. As I fuck her I bend my body down, pull some strands of her hair out of her eyes, turn her head, and kiss her lips, her face, her neck, anywhere I can touch. She clenches around me as I push into her deeper. This feels so dirty and so right at the same time.

I want more, though. I want to see her face and those perfect eyes as we fuck.

I pull out and direct her to lay on her back on the island. I hold onto her calves as I push back inside of her.

She feels glorious.

Bucking her hips up into me, she grinds her clit up and down on my cock.

She lets out a soft, escalating crescendo of a moan, and it spurs me on.

"Gonna come," I mutter, and I must sound like a caveman, but that's basically what I've become. I fuck her, animalistic, as my orgasm starts to hit. I can't control myself anymore. I smack the side of her ass, I pull her hair, I kiss her wherever I can, I push deep into her as I lose control.

"Oh God, yes," she mutters.

We tighten our grips around each other and I spurt deep in her. She leans her forehead against my chest.

"God damn," I mutter breathlessly when we're done. I pull out and grab a dish towel for us to wipe our juices off of each other which we share. Then I kiss her senseless on the lips, not wanting to let go.

"Brett, Baby. There's something I need to tell you."

"Oh yeah? Let me guess. You're still hungry." She winks.

"My soul feels satisfied, but yeah I am still pretty hungry." I laugh.

"Mine too," she murmurs.

"No, it's something else I want to talk about. Over dinner."

She squints and nods, some surprise in her eyes that I'm being surprisingly serious.

I help her get our dinner for two set up and think about how to proposition her for something that's more than our benefits situation.

I help her bring the steak and potatoes and banana bread out onto my back deck.

"I should put on some real clothes," she says.

"No baby. You shouldn't. In fact, I think this is going to be your new mandatory uniform at work," I joke.

We head to the back deck, which is awesome because it's surrounded on all sides by bushes, and we get to have privacy while still enjoying our meal outside.

We sit outside on my deck in the beautiful fall Blackwell night. Brett sits across from me, and looking at her you would just think she's wearing an apron, you wouldn't think she was naked.

"Do you have enough mashed potatoes?" she asks me, nudging the bowl in my direction.

"Yes, I think I do. I think I have everything I need, except do you want a drink maybe?"

"Sure." She smiles.

"I'll be right back." I head inside and grab a bottle of wine and two glasses. Before I head out to the deck again, I take a moment to watch her from inside like a voyeur. Brett gazes out over my backyard. She has a curious mind, the wheels of her brain are always turning.

I wonder what she's thinking about right now.

Beyond her hotness and her beauty, she just has that zest for life that makes a man want to step up his game. As I look out into the Blackwell sunset, the orange-yellow sky on the horizon, I know that's what I've been missing and that's why I need to tell her right fucking now. I step out onto the deck, the 'L' word practically bouncing from my lips. I've never told a woman that I loved her until now. I uncork the wine and pour us both a glass and sit.

"I had no idea what you would do when I gave you the keys to the house, and you did not disappoint." I say.

"Well, I aim to please, so I'm glad I didn't disappoint," she responds.

"Seriously though," I say as I pour the wine into her glass and into mine. "How did you come up with the idea to wear just an apron? I mean it's the sexiest thing I've ever experienced." I sit down and leaned back in my chair and a warm breeze wafts across my face. "That is just incredible. Your mind is so great."

"Is that your poetic way of saying that you think I'm smart?" she asks, batting her eyelashes.

"Yes it is, though I'm not poetic. You're the future New York Times Bestseller, so you should be the one using all the fancy words, right?"

She laughs.

"Hey," I say, as I reach my hand across the table. "I want you to know something, Brett. These past few weeks I've felt different. Every day I feel a little more different and I finally realize what it is that I need to tell you."

"What do you need to tell me? Just say it," she answers. Right as I'm about to let her know how I really feel, the doorbell rings. I roll my eyes; you've got to be kidding me.

"It's probably just telemarketers or something," I joke.

"Telemarketers, really? We don't have telemarketers in Blackwell and telemarketers don't ring doorbells."

"Oh right," I say. Well, it's probably just a window salesman then, I'm sure they'll go away." "Yes," I say, as I open the back door that leads out onto the deck. I clench up when I recognize the person.

It's definitely not a telemarketer.

It's Kim Murphy.

"Sebastian." She smiles, a little too snidely for my liking. "What are you doing with your door open and what the hell? I've been trying to call you all night and you haven't answered." I freeze. I can smell the liquor on her breath from here.

"I was on a plane."

"Oh," she replies.

"Who's there?" I can hear Brett calling from the deck.

"Oh, it's no one, just hang on." I go into my house and nicely try to defuse this situation which could get out of hand very quickly.

Five years ago, Kim and I shared a one-night stand.

It was a celebratory night, and then the next day we went back to being normal.

Sometimes though, the awkward face of that one-night stand shows its head.

At times such as right now.

Her weird streak of jealousy in the interview with Brett makes sense all of a sudden.

It was so long ago, and I thought we had both moved on. Apparently not.

"Kim, what are you doing here? I'm having dinner," I ask, my tone firm. I can smell quite a bit of alcohol coming from her direction.

"Well, you said last month how you were working so

much and you were a little bit lonely, so I decided I was going to surprise you and just come over so...surprise!"

She holds her hands out and smiles.

I rub my chin, trying to remember saying anything of the sort. Since I met Brett, I don't remember being lonely for a second. "Kim, I don't know what to say but, this is inappropriate."

"Excuse me?!"

"I'm busy tonight."

"Oh come on, don't act like you haven't been shooting me eyes when I come in for the projects that we're working on," she says. She runs a finger along her breasts, accentuating the cleavage that she has decided to show me here.

"Kim, I need you to leave. Right now."

"Oh, I have to leave because I'm an employee. Is that what you're saying? You don't date employees?" She takes a step closer to me and I can practically taste the whisky on her breath. I don't like it.

"No, I just mean you're a little bit drunk and I don't think this is appropriate."

"You act like we don't have a past."

"Maybe we do--a short one, a long time ago--but that doesn't mean you can come barging into my house like this. For the love of God, it was five years ago. Before you even worked at Blackwell."

"Who are you here with anyways?" she says and looks around. Fuck. I can still basically smell the sex in the air from when Brett and I did it in the kitchen.

After the many times we hooked up in the office, I won't let this be the way we get caught. *The first time we decide to hang out at my house.*

"Kim, I'm going to have to ask you to leave please, let's talk about this tomorrow."

"No, I'm not going anywhere. I want to hang out with you

and talk about the distillery project and how it's going. Who's here?" Kim rushes past me. I try to step in front of her but she sidesteps me and actually trots to the door that leads to the deck.

"No one, Kim, don't please." Kim runs out, and suddenly all I can do is spectate.

"Oh my gosh." She laughs. "Well, hello to you Miss Brett Blue." Brett's face turns ruby red.

"Hi Kim," Brett says sheepishly.

"Oh, wow, this is quite an amusing sight here." She crosses her arms and steps toward me. "The billionaire of Blackwell and his little hook up girl."

"Kim, I'm not going to say it again. Time to go."

"Oh, so now I see why you don't want me anymore, but you know what, I bet this is a sight that a lot of people would be interested to see." She takes out her phone as if she's going to snap a pic of Brett in only her apron but I step in front.

"Listen Kim, whatever you think about me, that's fine, but don't let it affect what you think about her."

"Oh yeah that's fine, but I'm going to snap a pic." Kim literally runs to the side of the deck, snaps a picture of Brett and I and heads into the house.

I start after her. I can hear her footsteps heading for the door.

"Kim, you don't want to do this! Why are you being like this?"

Almost at the doorframe, she turns back toward me for a moment. "Look, Sebastian sometimes a girl's gotta do what a girl's gotta do, it doesn't matter why."

"Give me your phone," I seethe.

"No," she hisses.

She leaves, heading outside and walking down the street. I want to stop her but there's nothing I can do. Short of physical force, I can call the cops, but what are they going to do? I rush back to the deck outside because no matter what happens here, any slandering of me, I don't care.

People can say whatever the fuck they want to say about me. They've been talking shit about me from the day I made my first dollar. What I won't tolerate is if they're talking shit about Brett. But when I walk back to the deck, she's gone. All there is are two plates with steak and potatoes and wineglasses sitting there untouched.

"Fuck," I yell.

A mix of rage and panic surges through me, and my heart speeds. I run back into the house and I hear something at the front door. I rush to it and see Brett in my foyer about to leave. The apron is on the floor, and she's fully clothed.

She opens the door, and there's just enough sunlight in the fading sky for me to see a tear rolling down her cheek.

"Goodbye Sebastian," she says. "Goodbye forever, asshole."

"Brett, just give me a minute! I can explain what just happened."

"You said you never slept with an employee. Sure seems like you and Kim share something. Chalk one up in the liar department."

"Kim and I were together one night, before she ever worked at Blackwell."

"Oh, so you slept with her and then you hired her. Well I'm glad you can get off on a technicality."

I block the doorframe so she can't leave. I've never seen her this worked up.

"It's more complicated than that. She was hired by a different department. I had no idea. We've come to terms with the night we spent together. It was just that--one night."

She shakes her head. "I thought I was special." She shrugs. "I'm not. Please, move Sebastian. I would like to leave now."

I hesitate, and then finally move aside.

As I watch her silhouette walk away, the sky seems to fade from blue to black in an instant.

This fall night couldn't be more gorgeous. I guess Brett and I were only mean to be a thing in the thunder and the rain, like our first night.

Worst of all, I never got to tell her the four words I'd been thinking about all night.

I love you, Brett.

CHAPTER 21

rett

IT'S LATE ON SATURDAY, and the locals of The Watering Hole are buzzing around us enjoying themselves. All I know is I'm getting drunk tonight.

Crystal takes a sip of her Pineappletini. I suck on the straw of my Long Island Iced Tea. Baseball highlights play in the background buzz of the bar, and the scene cuts to an interview of baseball's bad boy Jake Napleton.

I take another sizeable sip of my drink, unfocusing my eyes.

Crystal nods and processes the sob story I've just filled her in on.

"You can't trust any men. That's the moral of this story. Except for Zane and Lacy." She furrows her brow. "Zane didn't lie to Lacy, did he? He's a dick if he did."

As morose as I am, I can't help but smile a little. "I think I just wanted to believe that a billionaire playboy type like him could have a genuine connection with someone like me. But apparently, I was very wrong. But I'm not wrong about wanting another drink right now. Mason can you get on it? Shots here!" I nod toward the bartender and point to Crystal and I.

"I mean, that's all just too crazy to imagine. So, this Kim girl just came in and you heard everything?"

"Well, I heard her saying that she and Sebastian had a past when weeks ago Sebastian distinctly told me that he had never had an affair with an employee before."

"So Sebastian was lying."

"Right, and if he's lying about that one thing, who's to say he's not lying about lots of other things." I take a deep breath. "I admit the sex was so good. It was incredible, mind-blowing. I can't imagine doing that with anyone else but him."

"So he owns your pleasure?" Crystal says, stirring her drink.

"No," I quip back. "He doesn't own my pleasure...I just really like having sex with him. Fuck, I'm a bad person." I let out a sigh, and just in time, we're rescued by the bartender.

Mason puts the shots in front of us and we cheer greedily.

"To whisky!" I say, and we raise our shot glasses.

"To whisky!" Crystal smiles. "You know, I've stopped taking so many shots. But for you, for a friend in need, I'll take this bad boy down." We clink our glasses and both scrunch our faces as we take the shots down.

We slam the shot glasses back onto the bar.

"Well, I'm sorry you had to go through that, it seems really dramatic. Have you talked to Sebastian since then?"

"No, I say. I stopped answering his emails, and I blocked his number on my phone."

"Oh wow, taking extreme measures. You haven't done that since..."

"The one who shall not be named. I know. But I'm just done with him. You know me; what's the one thing I don't stand? What's my deal breaker?"

"Cheaters," Crystal affirms, because she knows me.

"Right, I'm sorry that's a deal breaker. If he's hooking up with this Kim Murphy lawyer chick on the side, I just don't think I can look him in the eye now."

"So you're going to go back to work right? Or are you a bestselling author yet?" she jokes.

I roll my eyes. "The book is fine. It's almost done."

"Glad you...finished it in spite of your lack of inspiration."

I take another sip of my Long Island. The book is exactly what I *don't* want to talk about right now. Sebastian was such a good inspiration, it's a pity he had to turn out how he did.

"Work is going to be awkward but I'll probably go back on Monday, it will just be very different and Kim knows, what if she tells other people in the office? Oh my gosh, I'm going to be like the 'office slut'. No, this isn't happening." I pound my fist on the countertop. "I never thought I'd be like 'that girl' and here I am, I'm 'that girl'.

"You're not that girl." Crystal shakes her head.

"Ok so, I know I just told you tonight but let me rehash it for you. I've been sleeping with my boss for weeks now and using him as inspiration to write the best romance novel anyone has ever written."

"Ok, so it makes you 'that girl' how?"

"I signed an NDA with him, which I'm breaking by the way to tell you this, so I'm not supposed to tell anyone I'm just hooking up with the boss behind everyone's back."

"Look," Crystal says. "I know you probably think this is the end of the world, but I mean there are a lot of guys; look around." I look around the bar; there are only two guys in the bar that aren't with girls and they're both playing pool. They're not super attractive. One has shaggy hair, the other one has a buzzed head. The only hot guy in the place is the bartender, Mason. And I've been noticing one of the waitresses shooting him looks all night.

"I appreciate your attempt at comfort, but there aren't a lot of guys as ripped and as driven as Sebastian."

"He really is ripped, huh?" Crystal asks.

"So ripped, I mean you wouldn't think it because he wears a suit a lot, but he's basically a cowboy in a suit."

"We can agree that we're not gonna talk about this anymore and focus on getting drunk." She nods.

"I can get on that pony and ride it late into the night." I laugh, half-heartedly. We clink glasses, drink, and laugh into the night and I try to forget that I'm in quite a pickle. Crystal gets up to go to the bathroom, and I stare into my drink. For days at the office; even just yesterday, Sebastian was fucking me senseless against his marble counter island. These are some of the most erotic experiences in my life and now what's going to happen to us? We're just going to not talk anymore? I take a sip of my Long Island and let the alcohol linger on my throat. Something tells me we're not over yet.

A few shots deep, the buzz starts to sink in, the alcohol flows through my veins and I feel good.

Crystal is off in the corner dancing with some cute young guy and I'm feeling a little bit claustrophobic and stuffy inside, so I head outside The Watering Hole into the open night air. I wave *hi* to the bouncer in on my way outside so he'll let me back in, and join the group of people standing outside — mostly smoking.

I don't join them in their cigarette smoking, instead I take in the night air, making sure to breathe upwind from the smokers. I look up at the sky, I can tell it's a cloudy night. In the distance, thunder rumbles and I'm reminded of that very first night I slept overnight with Sebastian in his office and how ridiculous we were together.

Together.

The word rings through me. What a shame we never truly were able to be together.

The implications of yesterday still haven't fully sunken in, or maybe I just can't process them. I don't know.

Maybe that's just how all men are, that's why I left my ex-boyfriend, only to find more or the same, well who knows?... I think about the story of Lacy and Zane. How their romance was just perfect. They were all hot, forbidden, sexy love in the office. It's just simply true that real love in the real world won't be matched by its love on paper because in books, there doesn't need to be any hurt feelings. I resolve to write a section of my book though, where Zane and Lacy take a horrific downturn, to at least match with reality to a point.

I take a deep breath wishing that the stars were showing tonight, but the clouded sky is quite appropriate for how I'm feeling, dark cloudy — the future ahead feels murky. I don't even know why I should show up for work on Monday, but I've still got to help my Mom pay down our debts.

Just when I'm about to head inside to the bar, I hear a voice to the side of me. I spin around.

"Hey there," the deep voice says.

I turn and see Sebastian standing there in jeans, boots, black T-shirt, and a baseball cap.

"What do you want?" I say crossing my arms.

"Brett, you just ran out yesterday. You didn't give me a chance to let you know what was going on. I want to explain."

"Explain what?" I say. "Explain how you've been having dueling romances with two of your employees at the same time?"

"Look Kim was drunk and that was incredibly weird and awkward. I'm sorry you had to go through that," he says. "But you've got to trust me on this, we haven't done anything in quite some time."

I step toward him enough that I can smell his cologne again. Even in the dark, only having the light of the moon and street lamps, he looks gorgeous as ever.

"You told me specifically when I asked you, do you do this with many employees? You said, no never, right?" I say.

"No never, as in, never any more. Look, me and Kim happened many moons ago, years ago. Since then, I've vowed not to be with an employee, past or present. But I broke that rule with you, it's true."

"So since we started hooking up, you haven't been with anyone else?"

I want to fall into his open arms but still something is holding me back.

"Since I've been with you, I haven't been with anyone else," he confirms.

I try to gauge if he's telling the truth. "I really want to believe you," I murmur.

He rakes a hand through his hair.

"Fuck, this is stressful. You realize I've been looking for you all over tonight?"

"And I've been trying to get away from you and not see you tonight after yesterday. I just needed some space."

We pause and there's an awkward air in between us. But the silence is broken by a hoard of women who walk on the sidewalk toward the bar, hooting and hollering in what looks to be some kind of bachelorette party. And guess who's leading the charge, but Samantha, a soccer mom who we sat with during the high school soccer game weeks ago.

"Oh my Gosh!" Samantha says as she runs up to us. "It's my two favorite soccer fans," she says enthusiastically. She's clearly drunk.

"How are y'all doing?" She hugs me and then hugs Sebastian, pushing her breasts into his chest just a little bit too much for my liking.

"Thank you so much for agreeing to meet up with me next week," she says to Sebastian. "You won't regret it and I'm going to be your next, best business investor, you'll see. And who knows, I could even be more than an investment." She winks, lays her hand on his chest, then draws it off. Sebastian's eyes meet mine, and I'm sure he must notice the daggers I'm sending him.

"Y'all headed inside?" Samantha asks cheerily.

I nod.

"Have a good night," Sebastian says.

The bouncer checks her ID and she heads inside.

"What the fuck was that?" I ask Sebastian.

"I have not talked to her for some time now. That's the first I've seen her since the soccer game."

"Yeah, well I wish I could trust you on that." I sigh deeply, and look at him. His eyes glisten in the moonlight. "Did you think we'd be more than this?" I stare down at my hands, and I'm suddenly heavy-hearted. "We were each other's fantasy on paper; nothing more, nothing less. I mean, should I really expect that a billionaire hung like a stallion is going to stroll into my life and make me his one and only? The problem isn't anything with you--it's that I wasn't realistic. So have a nice night, Sebastian."

He raises his voice to protest as I head back inside the bar. "Can't you at least let me *try* to explain?"

The buzz courses through me, and maybe I should give him a chance. But something inside me reverts to the very first time I shut down Sebastian. I spin toward him, put a hand on his chest, and stop him from moving forward, lightly touching his chest. And those damn muscular pecs.

Still, I resist him.

I flash my eyes up toward him, and maybe it's the way I

found out my ex-boyfriend Patrick was keeping five different girlfriends and I was just his Tuesday girl, when he let me believe I was *the one.*

"No," is the word that crosses my lips, and I swear I can feel a chill come over Sebastian's body. He swallows hard, but says nothing.

"Besides," I say, and look him dead in the eye. "You couldn't even give me *all* my fantasies."

As soon as I say it, I regret it, but it's too late. It can't be unsaid.

Even if Sebastian's in the wrong, calling out his lack of desire to give me a threesome is over the line.

He looks like I've just shot him in the gut.

In the distance, the thunder rumbles, and Sebastian turns and saunters away into the night.

I'm left with a slightly empty feeling in my heart. A tear rolls down my cheek, and I want him to fight for me. I want this to be different.

I want to be his one and only.

It's true. I'm in love with Sebastian Blackwell.

And I'm likely just one of many.

* * *

Monday at the office, the vibe seems a little bit off, and not only with me. Bob gets to work a little bit late and smelling of alcohol. I wonder if his problems are like mine and for the first time in a long time, I have some empathy for him and all of his creepiness. As creepy as he is, maybe he has some redeeming qualities about him. When I go into a meeting later that day for the cross-company task force I'm on talking about the construction of the new distillery, I'm surprised to find that Sebastian isn't the one running the meeting. On the other hand, Kim is standing there with a sly smile on her face as I walk through the doorframe.

"Hello everyone," she says. Troy follows me in.

"It's great to be here. Mr. Blackwell couldn't make it today. He had something come up. Actually, I'm going to be taking point on this task force starting now. The first order of business is, I'm going to have each one of you write a little synopsis about what you're actually bringing to the table for the task force. Here's a piece of paper." She hands out blank pieces of paper.

"Now, if you'll just spend ten minutes writing that out, we'll be able to get on with the meeting. Sounds good? Great," she says without waiting to see if there's a reaction from the audience. I sigh and Troy frowns as well.

"What the fuck is this shit?" Troy mutters next to me.

"I know, right?" I say. "Since when do we have to do such B.S. work. I thought this task force was supposed to be about efficiency." I get to work because Kim is barely out of earshot, so she might hear me and get me into even more trouble.

"Thank you, thank you, thank you," she says. "And sorry for the repetitive work, but Mr. Blackwell will be taking a leave of absence." There's a certain venom in her voice. Troy raises his hand.

"We didn't hear anything about this. Why wouldn't he tell us in person? Is he okay?"

"You know Troy, that's a good question and it's one that you don't need to know the answer to. Are there any other questions?" Something is super weird, but I can't figure out exactly what Kim did to Mr. Blackwell. She shoots me a deathly look.

"Perfect." Kim smiles.

"Now, I'll just be reading these to determine who will stay and who will go. Who is expendable and who is actually doing work. So, thanks for your time we're actually going to just leave it at that today."

She walks out of the room with the stack of papers in her hand, and this has just officially been the weirdest meeting I've ever been in.

CHAPTER 22

*S*ebastian

SOMETIMES, when the shit hits the fan in your life, you just gotta take a step back and think about things.

You also need to take some time off work, go out to your grandparents, and make some homemade pizza.

It's been a whole week since the fiasco with Brett. I've never been bent out of shape because of a girl before. Something about the way Brett and I left things sits horribly with me though, and I need to figure out what to do about it.

So on Friday evening, I head out to my grandparents' place, in the country to the north of Blackwell. Sure, I could go to my Dad's, but there's just something that makes me feel more comfortable asking my grandparents about this particular dilemma that I'm facing right now.

My grandmother kneads the dough for the pizza while my grandfather starts the homemade tomato sauce recipe that's been in our family for generations. It's really not that hard; olive oil, garlic, onion, and of course, the most important ingredient, fresh tomatoes directly from the garden. There's nothing like those. Tomatoes of the freshest order.

As I help my grandfather chop tomatoes, I am reminded of how tomato red Brett's cheeks got when Kim came to the door.

This has the dual effect of getting me worked up while putting thoughts of Brett back in my head, and also making me angry about my situation. I shake my head slightly, trying to get rid of the bad thoughts going through me.

"So Sebastian," my grandfather says. "What's got you down?"

"Just some work stuff." I shrug.

"Mo' money, mo' problems," my grandmother quips mindlessly, still kneading the dough.

I furrow up my brow. "Grandma...did you just quote Notorious B.I.G.?"

Before she can respond, my grandpa clasps his hand over my shoulder and squeezes. "Look Sebastian, now maybe you can bullshit your way with some people. But I know that you didn't call me up to take a day off work on a random Friday just because you want to make pizza with your lovely grandparents. Now, I know, we are great people. All I mean to say is you can go ahead and tell me what the hell is going on in your life. I may be eighty-five years old, but I give a shit about the repercussions of things. I'll give you the advice you need, no judgment."

I nod. "Thanks. I don't know if what I have to say is exactly appropriate."

He nods, and clears his throat, before turning to his wife of fifty-five years. "Hey honey, would you mind going outside and assessing the situation with regards to the weather. I was thinking we could eat outside but I want to make sure there isn't any rain coming."

My grandma turns her ears perking up. "Of course, Earl."

She gives my grandfather a kiss, then heads outside.

"All right Sonny, give it to me straight, no chaser," he says once we're alone.

"Well, see I did a thing with the girl at my company." I admit.

"Oh boy. Keep going." He tosssses the tomatoes I've chopped into the pot.

"Yeah, so this is probably kind of crazy, but this girl in my company was writing these fantasies during work hours about a woman and her boss. So I talked to her and turns out there was a bit of a mutual attraction there, to say the least".

"Mutual attraction." he smirks. "And you indulged in this attraction?"

"That's putting it lightly," I say, trying to figure out how to tell my grandpa that once Brett and I got started, we were banging like rabbits for the last few weeks. I tell him about Kim and how we hooked up one drunken night many years ago but how she still doesn't

seem to want to go away. And now is threatening Brett and us with going to the press with a picture of Brett in a sexy apron. This scandal of which wouldn't be great for my career, and it would certainly tarnish Brett's reputation in this small town forever and ever.

I tell him the story as concisely and best I can. Who knows how long my grandmother will be gone, and I'm just not sure how I would feel about her knowing all of these dirty details.

"Now back up a second," he says, holding up his hand. "And you say you were just about to tell this lovely lady that you are falling in love with her."

"The words were on the tip of my tongue right before everything went to shit. We didn't even get to enjoy our wine and the steak. My God, that steak was so juicy looking."

"All right, fuck the steak," he says, putting his arms down at his sides. "There's always another steak, but there isn't another girl. So if you could do something to get her back, what would you do?"

I finish chopping up the tomato and we put everything into the boiling pot of tomato sauce deliciousness.

I shrug, feeling a bit frustrated because it just doesn't make any sense.

"Hey Grandpa, let me ask you something. How the fuck can a guy like me make a billion dollars, but still have no fucking clue what to do when it comes to matters like these?"

He nods. "Well, I wish I could tell you. Seems like love is an easy thing when you've got it and a hard thing when you don't get it. But if I were you, just make sure she knows that you're serious about the whole commitment thing. Are you?" He raises an eyebrow. "I've known you to sow some wild oats."

"I am serious. I'm very serious." I swallow. "I don't think I ever wanted to commit to a girl and I always thought that just meant that I was a commitment-phobe. I mean, I've dated girls. I've dated lots of girls."

"Okay, okay", he says. "I know, no need to brag. You're a Blackwell, so of course you have."

I chuckle and a realization passes through me.

"But I think that the reason I wasn't wanting to settle down had nothing to do with me, it was just I hadn't found the right girl yet."

"So, what are you going to do? I mean you got to get her back somehow."

I shake my head. "She won't answer my texts, she won't answer my calls, she won't answer my emails."

"What is with you and your generation? Everyone is doing these E-Invites and emails. Whatever happened to the good old-fashioned way, where you just talk to them in person?"

I rub my face, stressed, but knowing he's right.

"So I should just go see her. But there's another problem. What do we do? Do I just announce our relationship to the world now? And what about the fact that there *is* no relationship now?" I shake my head. "Think about it, billionaire businessman hooks up with one of his employees as seen by this picture where she's wearing nothing but an apron. Grandma was right. Mo money, mo problems. Where is she anyway? How long does it take to…"

"She was wearing…nothing but an apron?"

"That's your takeaway from my whole rant? Can I have a beer?" I look in their fridge, but I only see milk and juice.

"Okay, gotta stop. That sounds pretty nice. The apron. Makes me think of back in the day when your grandmother and I used to--"

"Ahem!" I clear my throat as my grandmother walks back into the kitchen, a big smile on her face.

"I assessed the situation. And the weather seems a little bit cold, but I think if we put some sweaters on we'll be fine out there. It is about sixty degrees."

"Well that sounds fun. I mean I think eating outside is always better than eating inside. What do you say, Sebastian?"

"I say let's get this pizza going. It smells delicious!"

We finish making the pepperoni, as well as a vegetarian pizza because my grandmother is on a big vegetable kick. She's not one-hundred percent vegetarian, but she definitely prefers to eat a lot of vegetables.

Once the pizza is done, we head outside and crack a bottle of red wine.

The wine gets my grandparents going, and my grandmother gets that look on her face. It's the same look when she told us at Christmas last year all about my father's first-time drinking.

"So honey," my grandmother says. "Why don't you just tell *me* about what was going on in the dining room when Earl gave me the secret code to give you two some alone time?"

I scoff. "Did you just say 'gave you the secret code?' What on Earth are you talking about?"

My grandpa turns to me. "Oh come on, Sebastian. Do you really think I really need my wife to go out and check the weather outside? I've been living in this damn town for eighty-five years, I damn well know the weather," he jokes. "Plus, once the temperature drops below sixty-five, my knees ache like hell."

"You sly son of a bitch," I joke.

"So honey, why don't you just tell me what's going on? Sometimes you need a woman's touch you know, or a woman's advice, woman's perspective."

I hesitate, but the truth is I still don't have a plan of action for what I should do with Brett. So I give her the PG-13 rated version of what happened between Brett and me. She laughs when I'm finished.

"So what exactly are you afraid of here Sebastian? Are you afraid that everyone's going to know that you've been hooking up with this girl? Hooking up, right, that's what the kids are saying these days? Or shacking up?"

I practically choke on my wine, I'm laughing so hard.

"Grandma, well, first of all, yes, that's what they're saying these days and two yeah, yes, that's what I am afraid of. I mean, I'm a fucking billionaire. So I won't be hurting for money anytime soon, but like you always said, your reputation is priceless and I think after this gets free, everyone's going to be talking about how I am shady and how Brett Blue is some kind of office girl who gets around. And it's not like that."

"You love her though, right, don't you?"

I squint. My grandma and the light from the outside spotlight seep onto her face. She's seventy-eight, has grey hair, and I'll be damned if she still isn't one of the prettiest women I've ever seen.

"Yes, I do. I love her a lot, and how do you know about that, Grandma?"

"Well, it's just easy to tell. I can see it in your voice that you care about this girl and if you're not, let me put it this way. You wouldn't ask your grandparents to dinner to ask them for advice about a girl who you wanted nothing to do with. You see what I mean?"

"I do, but it's, can't you see how it's scandalous, Grandma? She's younger, and she's my employee. This could be against the policy that we're hooking up and once people find out about this, they're going to raise hell, I don't know, Twitter, Instagram. They will try to make me out to be some kind of a villain."

"Let me stop you right there," she says. "So you're going to have some--I think Kanye West likes to call them--'haters'."

I scratch my brow. "Grandma, you listen to Kanye West? And Notorious B.I.G.? I feel like I don't even know you."

"I've heard a few songs, don't worry about it. Anyways, the point is why do you care about some haters if you're with the girl you love?"

"She's literally my fantasy girl," I say. "She's the dream girl. I don't know how life would go on without her."

"Okay," she says. "I am going to stop you right there. Life will definitely go on with or without her, but I like seeing this side of you."

My grandma takes a big bite of her pizza, swallows it, and then chimes in again. "Look, you're a great man and you deserve a great woman and all these people can just, you know, they don't like it that you're in love, that's their problem. I mean, that's how I feel. How do you think I fell in love with Earl? I was a waitress, I was eighteen, he was a manager, he was twenty-five. Trust me, the other waitress girls were not happy that I was the one who got the big guy here."

"Big guy?" I frown my brow.

"They used to call me the big guy," he says. "Hey, don't ask questions. Anyway, you got enough advice here. I really want to just kick back and talk some sports, enjoy this pizza. Trust me, your problem is that your problem is a lot smaller than you think it is. You just gotta tell her the truth, tell everyone, and do your best to give her everything she wants."

"Give her what she wants," I repeat, thinking about the words as I say them.

There was only one thing I wasn't able to give Brett. At least, one thing that stands out.

I pour the wine and enjoy my pizza. My grandma's advice stays the best with me; sometimes you do just need a woman's perspective. Not to mention her blind faith in me.

I know exactly what Brett wants. Although it won't be simple to give it to her.

I glance at my phone, and I can't believe who I'm about to call. I love her enough that I've got to give her everything she wants. Even if she doesn't want a future with me.

"So this girl," my grandfather adds. "Do you love her?"

My heart swells at the very mention of 'girl' and 'love' in the same sentence, and my head fills with images of Brett.

"Yes." I nod.

My grandfather shrugs. "Sometimes you just gotta tell the truth. And then see what happens."

CHAPTER 23

rett

ANOTHER WEEK PASSES with no word from Sebastian. I feel stressed in a way, like we have something unresolved.

Monday, I go into work to find an email invite for a task force meeting later that afternoon. When I arrive at the meeting, Kim stands in front of us, her attitude as brazen as ever. She always seemed a little bit too cocky for my liking and something about her didn't sit right with me. It especially doesn't sit right after what happened on that fateful Friday night a week and a half ago. Before Kim begins to speak, Troy, who is sitting next to me at our table, flashes a smile my way.

"So, what's up?" he asks simply.

"Nothing much. Just work work work," I snicker.

He leans in and taps me on the shoulder with his pen.

"Work work work, huh? Look, I know there's more to you than work, Brett. And I want to learn about that other side of you sometime, if you'll let me." He squints at me, and I realize he's not a bad looking man. Especially the way his dimples look when he smiles.

Although I'm not going to be doing anything with a man anytime soon. Not after what I've been through.

Before I have a chance to respond to him, Kim starts talking to us.

"This is a very special week because this weekend, we are going to have a few of us going to Nashville for the annual postharvest conference. Has anyone heard of the fall postharvest conference?" she asks. I look around, not many people raise their hand. I do, because my family are farmers and we know about this sort of thing.

"Oh Brett, joy, you know about the postharvest conference fantastic. What can you tell us about it?" Her tone is disdainful, as if I don't have anything intelligent to say on the subject. I speak anyway.

"I went when I was six years old with my Dad. It was basically a bunch of farmers hanging out, having some cocktails--which I didn't understand at the time. I just sat by my father and listened to the live music."

My heart warms thinking of those old times with my father. The trip to Nashville was one of my first notable memories.

"Yes, that's pretty much correct. So, anyways, we are going to be picking a few of you to go and the instructions have come down from up high. Yes, Mr. Blackwell has instructed who will be going, and there will be three of you." My breath hitches because I haven't seen Sebastian since a week and a half ago. I wonder what he could be doing.

"The ones who are going to be going are..." she picks up a notepad. "Myself of course. Tro-oy," she says, as though it has two syllables. "Alena" she points at that girl to the side of me, the one who's an accounting specialist. "And ahh, Brett, you'll be going as well." My jaw drops because I was not expecting to be in this job and let alone, put into a task force.

"Oh hell yeah, Blue." Troy high fives me then grabs my hand and hangs on just an extra second too much. I sigh because Troy is a good-looking guy and he's not exactly my type, but that doesn't mean I would never ever consider going on a date with him.

But not anytime soon.

"So, ready to have some fun at this conference?" he asks.

"I guess," I mutter with a little bit of hesitation.

"Oh, come on, Blue. Let loose. What, you act like you got a boyfriend or something."

"Not exactly."

"Not exactly, huh? So, you have someone but you just don't know if he's your boyfriend?"

"*Had* someone," I correct, and then I realize I'm giving Troy too much information.

"Well, I think Nashville is a great place for you to have someone else." He winks.

WE ARRIVE ON FRIDAY MORNING, and spent most of the day at the booth. I talk to a lot of farmers about my own experiences growing up as a farmer's daughter. Big surprise, they're fascinated by me. As the day progresses, I enjoy myself, but I also realize I need to stay focused on work; which is kind of hard because everyone keeps talking about how Sebastian never misses this particular conference. When I think about Sebastian, my heart flutters, even though he has betrayed me from what I can tell.

I thought I could trust Sebastian, but in the end, who can really trust a billionaire playboy even if he was from your own hometown. I do feel bad for coming at him for something that wasn't really his fault, though. I mean, who am I to say "oh, you can't have a threesome with me" well, that's a hard line.

I more meant to just give him shit, but in my drunken state I don't know how it came out; probably harsh. It was more of just an excuse to push him away.

But that's my ultimate fantasy, that's what I thought about. I don't know where it creeped in originally, but it's there and it's not going away and if Sebastian and I are based on fantasies, well, he's going to have to give me it or was going to.

In my heart I know I wanted to be with Sebastian as more than my friend with benefits. And I loved him in a way that a school girl loves the unattainable. Sure, we'll never be together again, but a part of me wonders intensely what happened to him and where the hell he is right now. Why is he not at this conference that he always comes to?

The day passes and finally the nighttime hour arrives. We go to a team dinner with Kim, Troy, and all the other people. We eat in a fine Tennessee rib joint and by the end of it I feel full and decadent. My buzz courses through me.

"Well," Kim says, like a mother bird almost. "It's time for everyone to go back to their rooms."

When she says "their rooms" she looks specifically at me as though I'm a girl who's going to be up all night. I want to tell her 'listen, just because you happen to run into me in my apron does not mean that you know how I am all the time.' Instead of giving her any sort of look that will lead on what I'm thinking, I give her a blank smile; turning the corners of my mouth up, just slightly.

"Yes well, I have been known to have a good time especially at the Farmer's Conference," I say, and everyone at the table laughs.

Once the bills are paid we start to head out. Troy though, clasps me on the shoulder right as we head out the door and onto the street. I watch as Kim and the other girl get into a cab and drive off toward the hotel.

"Hey, you doing ok?" he asks.

"Yes, I'm fine."

"That doesn't sound very convincing. What the hell was that look between you and Kim? I saw that."

"It was nothing," I say.

"Hey, just come with me. Let's go grab a drink and think about some things. I want to ask you about writing."

My heart starts to beat a little bit faster.

How does Troy know about my writing?

I've mostly stopped working on the book at work, anyway.

"Writing?" I swallow. "What are you talking about?" He cocks his head just to the side.

"Look," he says. "Don't worry about how I know. But I know what you're writing and I'm just curious. It seems really unique and awesome and I want to get to know the writer side of Brett a little bit better."

"Umm, you know, I should just go back to my room. I really don't think this is a good idea," I say.

"I just want to ask you five questions about writing and then we'll head back to the hotel. This is not a date." He pauses. "I promise. Not a date."

"Not a date," I repeat.

"I don't know what you think but I just think you're really cool Brett and I'm not trying to hit on you here. Come on, let's just go up this rooftop place I've picked out and have a good time." My ears perk up at the mention of an open air bar.

"Did you say a rooftop?"

"Yes, I got a rooftop place scoped out. It's at one of those hotels just down the road." I take a deep breath and inhale the Nashville night air.

"I will go and have one drink with you," I say.

"One drink." Troy nods, and hails a cab.

Ten minutes later, we're on the rooftop of a bar overlooking downtown Nashville. The crowds are loud below us. A male and female guitarist play covers of popular country songs in one corner of the bar.

"I still don't understand how you know about the writing," I say. Troy slides his drink over to his side. Tonight, he's drinking a beer and I'm drinking a Mojito. Troy takes a swig of his beer, a local craft brew.

"Don't worry about how I know. But you really need to tell me about this writing thing and how you got started and all that. I'm curious."

My back stiffens; what on Earth am I supposed to tell Troy? That I half had an idea that I could write some sort of book and then I saw Sebastian and everything clicked and then Sebastian fucked me so well in every way, shape, and form that I couldn't not write the book?

Seems a little far-fetched if you ask me.

"Writing is just something that I've thought about since I was little," I say, giving him the stock answer. "And you have to tell me how on Earth you knew about my writing because I didn't tell almost anyone. I'm not dropping that."

Troy smiles only slightly, he leans in across the table.

"Now here's the thing," he says, his voice lower. "I don't want you to get freaked out about what we're about to do."

"What we're about to do?" My heartbeat quickens.

"Well, it will make sense in a minute." He taps the table three times and slides his beer to the end of the table, a cryptic gesture.

"Troy, could you tell me what's going on?" I say, suddenly panicked. I glance at the rest of the people in the crowd who are also on the rooftop, and when I see one particular individual, I freeze up like a deer in headlights.

Sebastian Blackwell stands in front of me, looking hotter than he's ever looked.

His jaw is firm as he stares straight at me, his eyes serious. He wears jeans and a T-shirt through which I can see his six pack quite well. Those very chest muscles that I pushed away outside of The Watering Hole.

I speak slowly.

"What the hell is happening?" I say as Sebastian walks toward me.

My palms sweat, my pulse quickens. Something about this scene just seems very, very off but at the same time, I'm extremely turned on all of a sudden.

"Sebastian," I manage to choke. "What is going on? Why are you here?"

"Why else would I be here?" he says, his voice low and cool. "You're here."

"I haven't seen you for a week and a half."

"Yeah well, you stopped answering my texts and calls, so I decided I would give you some space." His voice is low; lower than usual.

"Well, you didn't have to cut me off completely. I eventually texted you, I think." I reason.

He laughs.

"You think? Look Brett, you're amazing ok? You will never have any idea how amazing I really think you are and so, look, let's just not talk about this right now."

"Yes, I agree. Let's not talk about this right now." My eyes land on Troy. I'm about to cut in and ask him all the questions I'm currently wondering like, what the hell does Troy have to do with this? But Sebastian speaks first.

"Look, I own this bar."

"You do?" I say.

"Yeah, this was my childhood dream, to own a bar with a rooftop. So, let's go to one of the V.I.P. lounges where it will be a little bit more private." I look at Troy; his expression is calm, maybe a little bit nervous but he doesn't seem to be fazed by Sebastian and I's conversation which surprises me.

"Let's go," Troy agrees. We don't even pay, but Sebastian says it will be fine, so I follow him. We head over to a different section of the outdoor patio. We cut through and find ourselves in a certain corner of the place. There's a hot tub and a balcony over which we can see the entire city of Nashville; river and all. Some music drifts up toward us from a concert in a park somewhere. I freeze when I see the hot tub.

"Are we getting in the hot tub? I don't have a bathing suit."

Sebastian snorts a little.

"Look, you don't have to get in if you don't want to, we can just sip champagne on the side of the balcony or..."

"Yeah, we'll just sip some champagne here on the side," I say.

I stare at the hot water jets as they bubble.

"Or I can just get in and I'll dry off after," I say, suddenly bold.

Me. A hot tub. Two sexy men.

What the heck is happening?

Both of men squint at me, and to say I'm turned on is an understatement.

I start to feel like I'm Lacy in the final scene of Bossman with Benefits.

"I'll have some towels sent up," Sebastian says, and sends a quick text.

Troy looks on silently.

"Let's get into the hot tub, have some champagne, and enjoy this beautiful night." He's right, it is a beautiful night. It's 80 degrees in late fall, which is not always the case. The night air is hot-ish and crisp.

Troy takes off his pants and gets in in his boxers. Sebastian takes his off too, and submerges the lower half of his body while he's in his briefs.

I hesitate, and my hands are fidgety. I clear my throat to speak, but nothing comes out. I look at the two attractive men, both leaning back, viewing me in my floral dress.

"Screw it," I mutter to myself, and throw the thing over my shoulders. I take off my shoes, and slide into the water in my bra and panties.

Sebastian smiles, then reaches behind him. He hands each of us a champagne glass and fills it from his pre-opened bottle.

The champagne sounds loud as he tips the glass to pour, compared with how still the night air is in Sebastian's private rooftop.

He stares at me with those deep brown eyes, and I feel myself surrendering to him, in spite of everything we've been through.

"Brett, I know this probably seems weird, but we're cheers-ing to you."

"We are?" I ask, my voice a little shaky. I'm still trying to figure out what's going on.

"Yeah, we're cheering to your book that you've finished."

"How do you know I finished it? And for the love of all that's good, please tell me how and why this is happening. Sebastian, how did you know I was here?"

Sebastian tips his chin up, and again, the look he gives me sends me chills that reverberate through my entire body.

"Cheers," they both say, raising their glasses.

"Cheers," I echo.

I sit back, enjoying the feeling of hot water on my skin. It's a little bit too hot at first but once I'm in, it feels good and I'm pretty sure my drunkenness is amplified by the hot temperature. We clink our glasses together and take a drink, looking each other in the eye.

Sebastian takes a deep breath, and I know he's got something on his mind. I wonder if it's got anything to do with what's on my mind.

"Now that I've got you, I want you to listen to me. Right before you walked into my life, I was miserable. The truth is I only saw victories in business and sure, I had my ups but in general I was only after profit. I see things totally differently now and I know you say you can never be with me; that you can never love a man like me who is a playboy and I understand that. But that doesn't mean I don't love you. I always will love you."

I swallow down more of the bubbly, dry champagne, shocked.

Sebastian is using the L word.

For *me*.

"I'll take some more of this please," I say, holding out my champagne glass. This just seems awkward right in front of Troy; I don't understand it. Sebastian refills my glass. Troy sits still in the water. He's not super awkward, just curiously looking on at the two of us.

"I don't understand why you're telling me this now," I say. And I guess it's true what they say: A sober woman's thoughts are drunk woman's feelings. Because the next I know, I'm blurting out what's right up my sleeve.

"Why are you telling me this in front of Troy? I don't get it, Sebastian. I mean, you've always been a little mysterious to me, but this just makes no sense. How did you even know I was here?"

He takes a sip of his drink and glances out toward the stars, which are somewhat blotted out by the light pollution of the city and turns back to me, his eyes glistening in the night.

"See Brett, the thing is, you told me I could never give you your greatest fantasy."

"What's that?"

"Oh come on Brett, don't act like you don't know what's going on here. You said you wanted to have a threesome with two guys. Even if you don't love me, that doesn't mean I don't love you. And I want to give you everything you want."

He reaches out and tips my chin toward him with a finger.

"And when I say everything Brett, I mean fucking *everything.*"

CHAPTER 24

rett

"More champagne," I say after swallowing what I have in front of me. "Look Sebastian, I don't know what to say to that."

"You don't have to say a thing," Sebastian says.

My heart clenches and I twist it up in a knot. I look at Troy; he's got blond hair, a nice firm jaw. and his body is good and muscular; he's attractive. He's smart too, it's not like his personality is wanting for much. He's young. He smiles over at me and kinda of looks me up and down and then looks away, still a little bit shy about the whole thing.

"You want to do this."

"Look, it's probably a bit sudden. We don't have to do it tonight or anything or ever; whatever you want. Maybe it's seeming too real for you now. But I just wanted to put it out there and make sure you know. So I met up with Troy earlier this week, and explained to him the situation. Troy signed an NDA, too. We have an understanding."

He takes my hand in his; electricity surges through me, down my spine, through my legs and between them.

"Look, I will do whatever it takes to make you happy," he says. "I don't know if anything could ever be between us, but during this time I've always loved you. I think I started loving you from our very first kiss. And Brett Blue, you light a fire in me that I've never had in my life and I will do whatever it takes to make you happy. I don't give a shit what that entails and if this is your number one fantasy--"

"Ok," I cut him off.

"Ok, what?"

"Ok, let's do it. I want you both." When the words come out, suddenly I feel as though I'm on some kind autopilot; in a trance.

This isn't a fantasy any more.

This is about to become my reality.

Sebastian's hand is on the flesh of my leg. He squints towards me, those beautiful brown eyes, and I wonder what he's thinking. But that thought quickly dissipates.

"Baby," Sebastian murmurs in a throaty voice. "I don't care what the fuck you want now or ever, I'm going to make you the happiest girl in Blackwell and Nashville for that matter." I lean into him and our lips meet.

We kiss.

It's different now, butterflies surge through me starting in my lips, floating down to my neck and electrifying my heart. The kiss is hot but sensual, still sexual. A slight moan escapes my parted lips.

"Sebastian," I whisper.

"Yeah baby," he says.

"This is so fucked up, but in the weirdest, cutest way I

could ever imagine, this is the most thoughtful thing anyone has ever done for me," I say.

"That's right baby," he says, taking my chin in his hand and looking me in the eye. "And there's much more where that came from."

Sebastian's eyes dart toward Troy and he nods. Troy moves a little bit closer, sliding across the seat and sitting right next to me, his thigh touching mine in just his boxers.

"Hey," he says, cupping my cheek. "You okay with this? This is what you want right?" He runs a hand through my hair and his touch is soft, softer than Sebastian's in a way. "You seem shy."

"This is what I want," I utter. I think about all the nights I've spent obsessing, wondering how it would feel to be with two men at the same time. I can feel Troy's intense eyes on me. Sebastian's face looks savage, and I can tell he's ready to fuck the shit out of me. Sebastian plants another kiss on my lips and I let my tongue slide into him as Troy's hand falls to my knee. I feel another hand on my other knee; Sebastian, I can tell by the touch, even underwater. I feel Sebastian's hand ride up my inner thigh. My breath hitches; I feel so hot. So wrong, this is so wrong, but this is what I've wanted for so long. Sebastian's right. If he can bring me all my fantasies, he'd want to bring me this one too.

Sebastian kisses me harder; our tongues play hockey. A warm intense feeling washes over me like I've just been hit by a hot summer breeze on my forehead. I sweat and I feel Sebastian's hand running along my jaw bone.

"I love you, baby," he says. "I've loved you for so long and I can't wait to give you everything you want in this world, if you'll let me." His words are spoken soft, low, and true. He lets go of my lips, and I bite his lower lip as he falls away. I turn to Troy and look at his young face. I have no doubt his attraction is totally honest, that he wants me, and truth be told, he's an attractive man. He leans in for the kiss; I feel his breath as he hovers inches from me, not quite pushing forward. Not pushing his lips all the way onto mine.

"Wait," I say.

"Wait, what?" Sebastian says, suddenly concerned.

"I don't know if this is what I want," I admit. "I want you to give me everything but," I take a deep breath.

"Sebastian." I grip his hair over his neck. "I love you too. I love you and sorry Troy, I am not ready for this. It seemed good in theory, but all I want is this." I lean forward toward Sebastian, kissing him intensely. He devours my lips and I reciprocate.

Troy leans back and smiles and I'm impressed with the man for not being butthurt.

"This is what you want," Troy repeats.

"Yes," I confirm, and I can't believe Sebastian is willing to give me everything. Even when it's far out of his comfort zone.

Troy leans back, grabs for his champagne glass and smiles.

"You two are cute, I'm happy for you."

It's as if a bomb has exploded between Sebastian and I. The water splashes as he spreads kisses from my jaw, down my chin, to my neck, and back up. His hands explore me underwater and I ride mine up his abs, exploring his beautiful body at the same time. My eyes are closed but I hear Troy splash out of the hot tub. He must grab a towel and start drying himself off.

"I missed you," I mouth.

"I missed you too," Sebastian says to me. "Fuck, I want you Brett. I want you now, I want you forever, and I want you more than that. You understand how much I want you?"

"Yes," I whisper.

"Good."

"Hey," I say to him in a whisper. "I have one fantasy that I wouldn't mind doing tonight."

"Oh?" He arches an eyebrow.

"Yeah, it involves someone else, but not in the way that you think."

He furrows his brow, his face confused. I glance over at Troy, who is toweling off nonchalantly.

"Hey Troy," I say. "Where are you going?" He gives me that awkward look like 'I was just planning to get the fuck outta here so y'all could hook up.'

"Uh," Troy stammers. "You obviously don't want me here, so I'm going to be getting out of here."

"Hey," I say to Sebastian, lower my voice. "I want him to watch. Is that ok?"

"You want someone to watch us fuck?" Sebastian repeats.

"I do, I think it would be totally hot."

He nods after pausing.

"What do you think, Troy?"

Troy shrugs.

"I've come this far. Why not?"

Sebastian points to the corner. "Grab some champagne. Enjoy the show," he says, smirking.

Troy throws the towel over his shoulder and takes a seat in the shadows.

"So you want to be watched," Sebastian whispers. "Why?"

I blush a little and bat my eyes. Before answering, I maneuver to the corner of the hot tub and push the button to turn on the jacuzzi jets.

The humming sound buzzes through the air, a comforting white noise. Waist deep in the water, I straddle Sebastian as he sits in the jacuzzi with the hot water up to his chest.

The water is warm, and his body is even hotter, pressed against me.

"Because," I swallow, and he interlocks his fingers though mine, while staring straight through me, "I want to have the feeling of two men being turned on by me at once. I want to feel like I'm more than they can handle."

Sebastian throws his head back to the side, and under the water I feel him run his hand along my thigh.

He nibbles at my ear, and a chill runs through me.

"The way you scream when you're coming, you could turn on more than just two men."

I arch my neck back, and just the thought of more than one--whatever number it may be, has me so turned on I think I forget how to breathe.

Sebastian trails kisses down the side of my neck. I'm hyperaware of my breasts pressing up against his muscular chest. My skin tingles.

"And you think you can handle me?" I whisper, wondering if Troy can hear me.

Sebastian pulls his lips away for a moment and grips my neck hard, forcing me to look him in the eye.

"Did I handle you when I fucked you from behind in the elevator?"

"Yes," I admit, breathing deeply.

"And did I handle you when I screwed you on my kitchen island?"

"Yes, yes you did," I moan, melting into him.

"Right. And now I'm going to show another man *just how I handle you.*"

I feel my stomach swoosh with butterflies, and I ache for Sebastian. This newfound vein of possessiveness sends me over the edge. I want him *now*.

The water splashes around us as I grind back and forth against his cock in his briefs, feeling him through the wet fabric of my panties. He wraps his arms fully around me, plants another kiss on my lips, and undoes my bra.

I stand in the water, which is thigh deep on me.

He lifts his hips up and pulls down his briefs, exposing his cock. His hips hover just above the water, so his cock is the only thing still unsubmerged.

"Oh God yes," I murmur. "It's bigger than I remember."

He smirks, and stands up. Grabbing the sides of my panties, he pulls them down.

"Fuck, that's a nice pussy. I missed this," he growls as he slithers his hand down my stomach and lands a finger on my already swollen pussy.

The flesh of his throbbing cock bounces against my thigh, and I murmur. My knees shake, and one of Sebastian's large hands grips my ass, the other fingers me, and his eyes--those perfect brown eyes--stare right into me.

And I know no man has ever seen my soul as he has.

I reach my hand out and grab hold of his thick, throbbing cock.

My heart beats as his eyes sear into me, and I know he's what I want in my life to fill me.

Spiritually, and in *all the other ways, too.*

Sebastian takes me by surprise, growling as he lifts me up by my hips and sets me on the lip of the hot tub.

He spreads my legs and dives between them, licking and sucking my clit. Entering me slowly with two fingers, he curls them up in a 'come hither' motion. I lean back and clench against him, already on the brink of coming.

"You're wet already, Brett," he grunts.

"Yes," I breathe. "I'm wet...everywhere."

"Moan baby," he adds. "It's okay if you moan. This is my floor. Get as loud as you want."

I massage his head as he dives back between me, and his tongue makes me feel like the luckiest woman on Earth.

It's not like I needed his permission to let loose, but for an instant I'm reminded that I have an audience tonight.

I don't moan for my audience though.

I let go because Sebastian's tongue is golden.

Everything is warm, and wet, and swollen, and...

"Oh God!" I yell as I come, squeezing Sebastian's head. He's spurred on, and licks and fingers me even harder.

The orgasm intensifies and the pleasure ratchets through me. Lifting his head up from between my legs, Sebastian gets up off his knees and stands.

My jaw drops at his throbbing cock, still rock hard.

He leans into me and his lips graze my cheek just barely. "That was the hottest noise I've heard in my life," he says.

"Holy fuck Sebastian. I need you inside me. Now. Right now."

I stand up in the water, and we're both a little less than waist deep. He spins my body around. I lean down onto the lip of the tub.

He spreads my cheeks, and I feel the flesh of his tip spread me apart.

"Yes," I mewl. "Just yes."

"Aw fuck, that feels good," Sebastian growls as he pushes inside me, one pleasureable, filling inch at a time. Once he's all the way inside me, he just holds the pose for a moment, and I feel so complete with him inside me.

So completely full, that is.

As he thrusts into me, I brace for the slap of his hips against my ass and it feels so hard, so dirty, and so damn good.

Suddenly, the foam jets turn off, emphasizing the silence. All that can be heard is the *slap slap slap* of our wet bodies colliding together as I come again and moan.

"Oh God, Sebastian. Just like that. Oh God. Yes. Right there. Oh fuck."

After a few minutes, I feel so damn good I'm about to

come again when Sebastian pulls out of me, leaving me with a gaping emptiness between my legs.

Sebastian sits on the lip of the hot tub.

"Straddle me, baby."

I do as he says, and the position is a little awkward at first, because I have to squat partially in the water while still facing him.

"Is this right?" I ask, doing my best to think while still in a haze from my orgasmic state.

"Just like that. Keep sliding up and down on me. We'll find our rhythm. Yeah, that's it. Oh fuck, Brett," he groans, as I bounce up and down on him. Grabbing my hips, he helps me find just the right rhythm, and the water splashes in the hot tub as I bounce up and down on his cock.

"Gonna...fucking...come," he snarls, and I ride him hard, my ass cheeks slamming into his hips. He grips my ass and pushes me down onto his cock as he shoots his seed deep inside me.

When it's done, we're both panting. I lean forward and he laces kisses on my ultrasensitive breasts and neck.

"I've never done it in a hot tub before," I utter. It's a basic statement, but right now my mind is devoid of most logic.

I stand up and sit on the side of the hot tub. He lays back on the wooden deck, and I rest my head on his chest.

"We're going to be doing that a lot," Sebastian says. "I can't wait to tell everyone about you."

"Everyone?" I say, pushing my head up on his chest so I can see his face.

"Yeah. I want the world to know you're my girl, Brett. If you're okay with it, that is."

When he says those words, my heart feels full.

"I am."

"I'm not saying we're going to get married now or

anything Brett, but I love you. I've never loved anyone like this. I can't wait for what the future holds."

"Me neither," I whisper.

For a few minutes, we just lay like that, until there's a sound behind us.

"Well, I think I'm going to get going," Troy bellows. We both jerk our heads around. I'd been so into the moment, I forgot he was even there.

"By the way. You two are hot as fuck when you fuck. That's all."

Troy leaves. I hear his footsteps on the deck as he walks out. I fall asleep like that, smiling in Sebastian's arms.

CHAPTER 25

ebastian

ON MONDAY MORNING, I'm so jovial, it's appalling.

I whistle when I'm shaving in the morning. I whistle in the car ride to the office.

When I see my secretary, I'm still whistling. I've got a permanent smile etched into my face.

"Morning, Fiona!" I smile as I whistle my way into the office.

"Morning, Sir!" She smiles back. "Someone's in a good mood today."

She's right. I'm as giddy as a schoolgirl.

After this past weekend, my head's spinning. I finally feel like Brett and I are on steady ground, to say the least.

"I am indeed. I'm back and ready to crush this week."

"Good. We missed having you here."

"Call an eight thirty meeting. Company-wide. We'll do it

in the Bristol Conference room that can seat two-hundred. I have an announcement to make."

"Eight thirty? Sir, that's in less than a half hour."

"Yes. It's a very important announcement. Send an all staff email and make sure everyone knows it's mandatory."

"Yes, Sir!"

I straighten my tie on the way into my office, and slide my hand over my abs, which feel like I spent the past two days doing some intense CrossFit ab camp.

Maybe I've discovered a new workout plan to maintain my six pack:

Sex-fit.

I chuckle.

I lost count of the number of times we made love this weekend. I'm still dizzy from all the banging.

And I've got endurance. If my ab muscles are sore, I can't imagine how Brett must feel.

We couldn't keep our hands off each other after the flood gates opened up.

I sit in my office chair, do a one-eighty spin, and look at the town below me. Blackwell, the greatest small town on Earth.

Blackwell, named for one of my great-great-grandparents, and the well they started here.

As I gaze out into the late fall, I wonder what my ancestors had to do to accomplish their dreams. Every generation has a different challenge, and my generation is no different. Whereas my grandparents seem to have made a simple choice to be together, my choice seems so much more complicated. Maybe it's the fact that it seems like, in today's digital world, there are just so many options out there.

I stand up, cross my arms, and my lips quirk just slightly upward in a soft smile. All of a sudden, it makes sense why my grandparents were able to stay with each other all that time. It wasn't that they learned to stand each other, it's that they couldn't stand life without each other.

And now that I've found that person for me, I need to let everyone know.

My phone lights up, and I quickly grab it, expecting a text from Brett.

Adrenaline pumps through me when I see it's from Kim.
What the fuck does she want?
Kim: Hi. So you're back at the office today
Sebastian: Yes. Why?
Kim: You're done. I'm sending those pictures
Sebastian: Why are you doing this?
Kim: Why wouldn't I do this? I'm not just going to sit back while you play some random employee

My blood vessels tighten, and fuck if I'm going to let Kim talk that way about a girl who could very possibly be my wife in the future. Plus, communicating over text is damn near impossible.

Sebastian: I called a meeting for eight thirty, let's talk after
Kim: You didn't pay me. If I don't see that money in the next thirty minutes I'm forwarding it to all of the employees here.
Sebastian: Is this about the money or the morals?
Kim: Just do as I say, and then maybe you won't end up the latest billionaire laughing stock of the country

Kim forwards me a chain of photos. She took a few, all of Brett, sitting in just her apron at the dinner table next to me.

In each photo, Brett looks absolutely stunning. I wish I

could take a moment to admire them, but right now, I need a plan to squash Kim.

I take a deep breath, and try to stay calm. I clench my fists, and feel my blood boiling over.

When the hell did Kim get so vindictive? She's been doing such a good job here, that I haven't even been supervising her much when it comes to her job.

I run my hand on my chin and think back to the new hires, and my heart races at a realization.

For all of the interviews I've done in the past couple of years, Kim has only found it necessary to 'randomly sit in' on the female candidates.

Is she...weirdly jealous of them?

I glance at my watch, and it's time to head to the Bristol room so I'll be able to make it there in time for the meeting.

As I walk, I formulate a plan so crazy, it just might work.

My grandfather's words ring in my ear.

Tell the truth, and let it kill you.

I press the elevator door to the sixth floor, where the meeting room is. I feel a rush as I step into the elevator. I'm ecstatic. I'm nervous. I'm seething with anger. All at the same time. I barely sense the people around me in the elevator.

The world around me is moving in slow motion.

When I get to the meeting room, about half of the chairs are filled.

I step onto the elevated stage, which puts me about a foot and a half above everyone.

My employees settle into the room, and once the time hits eight thirty, they quiet down.

I notice Kim file into the back, just as the doors are closed.

She smiles devilishly, and taps her phone three times, then rubs her thumb and forefinger together in a 'show me the money' motion.

Brett arrives late, and my heart pounds like mad at the sight of her. Today, she sports a white dress with a pink cardigan. We make knowing eye contact, and I realize I probably should have texted her to let her know what I'm about to say. Or talked it out with Brett beforehand.

But Kim's threats bring Brett and my situation to the forefront.

I tap my heart a few times, and hope she'll understand what I'm about to say.

"Thank you all for being here," I start. I gesture as I speak. "I know Monday morning meetings are rough, especially when they are impromptu. But I called you all here for a very important reason. At this time, I need to address the more personal side of being an owner and a businessman in a small town."

I notice Bob files in late, and takes a seat right next to Brett. For some reason, that puts me on edge. Reading Brett's face, she looks slightly uncomfortable.

I clench my jaw.

"Anyways, today I want to talk to you all about the benefits we all get from being part of this company. You've all been so great, that everyone here, in this room, I am giving a raise of a thousand dollars per year, effective immediately."

There are a couple of "wooo's" from the crowd, and a few claps. Troy, who is sitting in the first row, lets out a whoop.

"Hell yeah, Mr. Blackwell!" he says, with a knowing smile. "Someone's in a good mood today!"

"I am in a good mood," I continue, speaking clearly. This next part of the speech is where the rubber hits the road, and I need to make sure I'm on my game.

"Because I'm in love," I say, flat out, and nod with a smile to a crowd whose jaws fall open. The crowd goes silent.

"Over the last couple of months, I started something that

I vowed I never would. And something that's forbidden in the company's handbook, explicitly."

I glance at my HR guy, who's sitting in the front row, eyes wide.

"I went and fell in love with an employee," I say, and the crowd gasps, then starts looking around and chatting with each other. "Silence!" I clap my hands a few times and they pipe down.

I look over at Brett, and her face is stark white, but she's not even paying attention to me.

Bob has his arm on her shoulder, and she's sinking further down into her chair to avoid him touching her.

"I hired her. And then I fell head over heels, right in love, with Brett Blue."

Bob makes eye contact with me, and slowly removes his hand from Brett's shoulder.

"Brett's my employee, yes. And I tried my best to resist her. I didn't want to fall for someone at this company, because it's damn complicated. But I did. So now, here we are, and I'm confessing this to all of you, because I want you all to know why your Boss is the happiest guy in the company today."

Troy stands up. "Hell yeah, Mr. Blackwell!" He starts a slow clap.

The crowd gets into it, and after a few moments, they break into full applause.

Brett stands up. "It's weird, and it's true. Sebastian and I are in love."

Kim runs up from the back, clamoring down the aisle.

"Yeah! True love, that's what you call it!" she yells as she gets to the front row, and stops in front of the stage.

"Alright people, listen up. This is all a bunch of bullshit, I'll have you know. You want to know what Mr. Blackwell and Brett are really up to?! Let me show you."

I watch as Kim presses a couple of buttons on her cell, and seconds later everyones' phones buzz in their pockets.

Mine does too.

I pull it out and swallow as I look at the image. It's Brett, in her cute as fuck apron and nothing else. In the picture, she has some serious side boob, and I wish this situation were less stressful so I could take some time and admire her.

"See?" Kim yells to the crowd. "*That's* what you call love? I mean come on," she scoffs. "When two people are in love, they don't get naked and cook dinner. That's just not what happens. This is a clear sign of-"

"Shut. Up." The voice comes from the middle of the room. It's Brett's.

"Exca-use me!?" Kim yells, her voice shrill.

The room is dead silent with the exception of the two ladies.

"Enough!" Brett continues, weaving her way out of her row of chairs. My veins tighten, not knowing what she'll say, as she makes her way to the front of the room.

"I'm sick and tired of sitting here and listening to this crazy person try to blackmail us. It's true. Sebastian and I have had a thing going for some time now."

All of the jaws in the room are agape.

"Sebastian and I have a connection--a really great one. And who are we to deny that just because he's my boss?"

Kim runs in front of her, huffing like a mad woman. This whole thing is unfolding like a spectator event in front of my employees. Of course, this is better than if Kim had gone straight to the press with that picture.

Whatever happens now, we're coming out with the truth.

My grandfather's words ring in my ear again, and I know we're doing the right thing by telling the truth right now. No matter how big the pit is that's forming in my stomach right now.

As Brett nears my area on the podium, my heart warms by her mere presence.

In the face of a possible crisis, with the entire company staring at her, she smiles with confidence.

"Look," she says firmly, taking the mic. "I'm not going to let you people who live in glass houses sit up and judge me. You're all going to act like you haven't ever done something freaky fun for love? Like getting dressed up in just an apron to make dinner for your man?"

Everyone's eyes seem to widen in the crowd.

"Fuck yeah!" Troy says from the first row, pumping his fist in the air. "That's the kind of girl I want when I grow up!"

The crowd chuckles a bit, and I do too.

"When I met this man seven years ago," Brett continues, "he defended me. I don't have to go into that story now, but two months ago, he dropped into my life again. To be honest, at first I thought he was a cocky asshole, and I didn't really want to be with him. But for all of you who haven't been as lucky to spend time behind the scenes with this man, he's not an asshole. He's actually the type of man who will give someone he loves anything they want. And when I say *anything*, I mean absolutely anything at all."

She turns to me and winks.

Our hands knock together at our sides, and I take her hand in mine, interlocking our fingers. "Let's not go over all the details," I whisper to her.

"This doesn't change a damn thing!" Kim yells as she power walks to the front of the room. That's when I notice Kim already smells like liquor.

Uh oh. I think someone might have a problem.

"If you do not promise that you and her will never be together, I'm going to unleash this photo on social media and give it to all the employees! Imagine the headlines! 'Small town business owner has kinky affair with employee.'"

Brett looks over at the picture and nods. "Hmm. I like it. I look pretty hot in that apron. I think you've actually gotten my good side. Here, let me do it."

I'm astonished by Brett's honesty and boldness. This is a side of her I don't really know.

She snatches Kim's phone from her hand, and with a few quick motions, she forwards it to the entire employee list.

All of their phones buzz collectively, and they all take them out and look at the very sexy picture of Brett.

Kim grabs her phone back, her tone worrisome. "No! You can't do that! I'm blackmailing you!"

Brett shrugs. "No, you're not. Because, I don't care anymore! Show that picture to anyone you want. Big deal."

I let my hand slip to Brett's waist as I inhale her sexy, peachy scent. God help me, I'm so in love with this woman. And I'm so damn happy.

"Baby," I say, turning to Brett. "You know what I think of all the stuff that has happened between us in the last couple of months?"

"What?"

"I think we need to do more of this."

I lean down and kiss Brett on the mouth.

The crowd erupts in applause.

I kiss her harder, egging them on.

All of the employees stand up, and their applause gets louder.

"No. No!" Kim raises her voice above the volume of everyone who is clapping.

"Kim," I say, when I'm finished with my kiss. "You're fired. Pack up your things, and get out of here." I dial my phone, calling Fiona, and tell her to send security to escort Kim out.

"Hey, Brett," I say as the applause still echoes around us. "Tell me, how exactly does that book of yours end?"

"I'm not sure. I haven't come up with the official ending yet."

"Alright. Well let me know if you want to act out any more of those scenes, baby."

"Of course."

Security arrives and takes Kim out.

"Alright everyone," I say, taking the microphone again. "Let's get back to work. I love you all very much. But especially you, Brett," I wink.

"Yeah, fuck yeah! Sebastian's the man!" Troy yells and does a couple more fist pumps. He winks at me and Brett. Troy and myself exchange knowing glances between us.

Troy's a stand-up guy, and I wish him the best.

The crowd gradually spills out until it's just us again.

Everyone's gone now. We kiss again on the podium, and electricity shoots through me.

"Brett, you know what I like the best about this, all this?"

"What?" she murmurs, looking up at me with her gorgeous blue eyes that I can't wait to stare at for the rest of my life.

"You were so ridiculous today, you made me realize something big. You're just the right kind of crazy for me."

CHAPTER 26

rett

Three months later

It's a brisk Friday night in February. Sebastian has been driving me around for what seems like forever, though he won't tell me where we are going.

"Are we there yet?" I ask, adjusting the blindfold and taking a deep breath. I'm tempted to reach up and remove it, but I don't.

"Almost," Sebastian says, and I swear I can hear him smirking even though I can't see a thing.

"Seriously, where are we going? I feel like we've been driving in circles forever."

Sebastian laughs, and I wiggle in the front seat of his truck.

"Don't worry about it, baby. Don't you trust me? After all we've been through."

"Yes, of course, but I just like knowing where we are headed."

He reaches across from the driver's seat and pats the skin of my thigh.

It's a cold February night, but I insisted on donning a black skirt. Lucky for me, Sebastian's truck has a new feature: heated seats with a self-massaging feature.

"I just want to make sure you are good and surprised for dinner tonight. This is a special celebration for your book coming out this weekend."

I lean back and enjoy the heat of the chair warmer on my body.

"At this point, we could be on a plane back in Nashville by now."

The truck jolts to a halt, and I hear Sebastian put the engine into park.

"We're here!" he exclaims. "Don't move yet though. I need to do something."

"What now?"

He reaches across and I feel him unbuckle my seatbelt. "You look gorgeous tonight," he whispers in my ear, his voice grizzly.

"I wish I could see you to tell you the same. But you know, I've got this."

"It's okay. You can feel this."

He guides my hand to his bicep, and I feel the hardness of his muscle over his jacket.

"Have you been doing extra pull ups in the morning?" I exclaim.

"Nah," he answers. "I *have* been doing a lot of cross training on the weekends though."

"Cross training? You're gonna have to tell me about that."

"Oh. Let's just say it involves keeping my body hovering above a certain someone as I do a lot of this."

He leans in and surprises me with a soft string of kisses that start at my neck and work their way up my jawline, until he lands one on my cheek, and finally puts one on my lips.

I moan softly and my whole body tingles. I squeeze his arm, and the fact that I still can't see a thing enhances all the other senses.

He drags a single finger from my ear down to my chin and kisses me once more.

"Not fair," I breathe. "You're getting me all hot and bothered and we haven't even gotten to the actual date yet."

"Oh, I'm sorry. Does it turn you on when I do this?" He kisses me softly on the lips again and slips a hand between my thighs, running it ever so gently closer to my panties.

"Sebastian," I whisper, my legs quivering. "I'm getting so turned on."

"Shit, sorry babe. I need to show you this first."

"Don't lie. You're not sorry you turned me on."

"Okay fine. Sorry I'm not sorry. But I *do* have to show you something."

He removes the keys, and gets out of the door on his side.

Walking around to my side, he opens my door and takes hold of my hand, helping me out of the car.

Outside now, I can hear a few odd people chatting in the night on the sidewalk. My heels click on the concrete as Sebastian guides me across the street. Taking hold of my shoulders, he turns my body around. I keep my eyes closed underneath the blindfold.

"Can I please see now?"

"Wait. Keep your eyes closed just a minute more. I'm going to take off the blindfold and then cover your eyes with my hands."

I do as he says, and he stands behind me while he covers my eyes with his hands.

"One. Two. You sure you're ready?"

"Yes! For the love of God just show me what it is."

"Three," he says as he lets his hands drop to my waist. I open my eyes, and I'm nearly blinded by the red, yellow, and blue neon lights of a big sign in front of the brick building that was formerly Blackwell Country Pizzeria. My jaw drops in awe at the new wording of the sign.

Instead of saying BCP, it says *Blue Pizzeria*.

"Oh my gosh. It looks amazing!"

I spin around, still in Sebastian's arms.

"I thought it was appropriate since we had our first awkward encounter here."

I shrug. "I was pretty awkward back then. I'll give that to you."

"Smart. But awkward. Come here, Blue." I get on my tippy toes to kiss him, and adrenaline pounds through me.

"So are you ready for dinner?"

"Sure!" I say. "I'm starving."

"Good. We've got a lot of celebrating to do for release weekend for your book."

I hold his arm as we cross the street. Sebastian holds the door open for me. "After you, my lady."

"Oh, you're such a gentleman," I say, glancing over my shoulder. "More guys should—"

My thoughts are interrupted when I notice that there isn't a single sound coming from the restaurant on a Friday night. It sounds suspiciously silent.

I whip my head around and see banners draped throughout the restaurant that say *Congrats, Brett Blue, on your book release!*

"Um, Sebastian, what is—"

"Surprise!" shout a dozen or so people as they jump out

from behind the bar, and from various pieces of furniture throughout the restaurant.

"Holy crap," I mutter, as well as a few other expletives, and I literally jump up when I see them all.

"What's this for?!" I ask, turning toward Sebastian.

"Your book releases tomorrow. You put so much work into it. So I invited your family, friends, and some of my family here to celebrate."

I see the faces of my good friends and family. My mom, sister, Crystal, and Crystal's little sister are all here.

"Wait. So Mom, you knew about this all along?"

"Macy told me."

"Oh my gosh." I stare at Macy. "I thought I was doing a good job keeping this book a secret. Apparently not."

Crystal's little sister shrugs. "My mom says I can't read your book until I'm eighteen. But I like the pictures you are putting up on Instagram. And that cover? So hot. I wanna be an author someday. And knowing that Macy's big sister became an author? That inspires me to think if you can do it, I can do it too."

I meet Sebastian's mother and father, too, as well as his brother Liam and his girlfriend.

Sebastian's grandparents are there too.

For a while, we mingle and have drinks, and I'm peppered with questions about the new book. I answer questions as best I can, and everyone pulls up my Instagram and ogles the cover model. Finally, we sit down to eat pizza.

"Bossman with Benefits," Crystal says, holding a slice in front of her face. "However did you decide on that topic?"

Sebastian chimes in. "We'll never know," he says sarcastically, wiggling his eyebrows. "This book will go down in history as being totally made up. Historians some day will try and figure out how Brett came up with the idea."

I push Sebastian's shoulder, and my face goes a little red.

"You know, I don't think it's necessary to talk about where I got my inspiration. I'll just let you guess for yourself."

"What I want to know," my mom adds, "is where you got such a sexy cover model. I hear they are expensive.

My hand finds Sebastian's leg under the table, where no one can see what my hand is doing.

My mom absolutely doesn't need to know that I asked Sebastian to be the cover model, and then cropped the picture from just above the mouth to make sure no one would recognize him.

"Ah, I'm not sure," I say, pretending to squint off into the distance. "I think my cover designer found him on some random site or something."

"I swear I've seen that guy before somewhere," Crystal says, staring at me as she shovels a piece of pepperoni pizza into her face.

Sebastian's hand meets mine underneath the table, and he squeezes it. It's a small gesture, and it's not erotic, like so many of our adventures have been. But there's something about the way he does it. Lightly touching my hand, he runs his middle finger back and forth on my palm.

He sends a chill through my entire body.

Sebastian changes the conversation topic away from my book, and refocuses it on my sister's offseason soccer training regimen. I take a deep breath and space out for a minute, remembering that fateful night years ago when an asshole customer went off on me for some pizzas that didn't get delivered.

Sebastian had my back then, and he has my back now. I originally thought I might feel embarrassed to tell my friends and family I'm writing *those* books—the ones where blow jobs are described in full and no details of sexual encounters get away.

With Sebastian at my side, stroking my hand, I feel so

liberated and so lucky to have a man who is cocky on the outside but a humble country boy at heart, and who supports me no matter what kind of crazy ideas I come up with.

The corners of my lips curve upward in a slight smile, and I rub his forearm. To my left sits Sebastian's grandparents, and as I glance at them I notice something. His grandmother rubs her husband's arm in the same way I'm doing right now. It's not an erotic gesture necessarily, but it warms my heart deeply.

"Brett? What do you think about that?"

I'm jolted out of my dream, and Sebastian's brother Liam is asking me a question.

"Think about what I just said. You write romance novels. What's the key to a long-term relationship?"

I look at Sebastian, and he smirks at me, awaiting my response.

I shrug, glancing around the table at all of the faces who are eagerly awaiting my response. I think back on Sebastian and my torrid romance that started out as just friends with benefits and evolved into something so deep I still have a hard time totally defining it. A smile crosses my face as I picture myself wearing nothing but an apron and cooking Sebastian dinner.

"Sometimes, you just gotta get a little crazy."

Sebastian wraps his arm around me. "That you are, Blue."

As I fall into his arms, I notice his grandmother is smiling ear to ear at me. She winks.

"The Blackwells always fall for the crazy ones," she says, and I don't know if that's a dig or a compliment.

"I'm just happy I know I'm with a man who will go above and beyond to make me happy. He'll do everything. And I mean *everything*."

Sebastian and I squeeze hands under the table, and I wonder just what our *everything* will be in the future.

HOW TO GET THE BONUS EPILOGUE

I also wrote a bonus epilogue/short story. It's called: *Two Sebastians are better than one.*

Yeah, it's exactly as it sounds. It's one of the hottest things I've ever wrote.

I want to send it to you! When you're done just follow these simple instructions:

1) Make sure you're signed up for my mailing list. Just go to

mickeymillerauthor.com

2) Reply to my mailing list confirmation (or any email I've sent you if you're already a subscriber) with a link to your Amazon review for Boss with Benefits!

3) That's it! I will send you the story via email.

Thank you for reading!

XO,

Mickey

ACKNOWLEDGMENTS

This book is dedicated to my support network of fellow authors, editors, beta readers, fans, and friends who have supported me from day one when my first book, Playing Dirty came out last November.

For reasons I won't go all the way into...this book was extra special, and I'm so happy to bring it to you all.

Thanks to all of the Misfits, to my editor Dani and to my beta readers Barb, Leddy, Lauren, Becky, and Virginie. And to Megan.

And thanks to those who I've met along the way. No matter how small or large we feel, there is no denying we are all nodes with the potential for a ripple effect that extends farther than we'll ever know.

Lots of love,

Mickey Miller
    www.mickeymillerauthor.com

ALSO BY MICKEY MILLER

Blackwell After Dark - Small Town Romances

Sports Romances Series - Ballers

Playing Dirty

The Casanova Experience

Mickey Miller books cowritten with Holly Dodd:

Dirty CEO

Hotblooded Prizefighter

Subscribe here to my email list here so you don't miss out on any new releases! All of my releases are 99 cents for the first few days: http://eepurl.com/cjHaxD

The final book in the Blackwell After Dark Series

Stay tuned!

Join Mickey's Facebook Group for live feeds and reads. Just search "Mickey's Misfits" on Facebook!

Before you go…here's a sneak peak of a favorite scene from another one of books, the Casanova Experience.

Made in the USA
San Bernardino, CA
23 July 2018